A TREASURED LITTLE MURDER

A VIOLET CARLYLE HISTORICAL MYSTERY

BETH BYERS

For Ethy

SUMMARY

August 1926

Jack and Ham's first solo case is placed on pause just as the tale of a treasure is brought to light.

As the case progresses, Vi and Rita dive in, and somehow it becomes a competition between the two couples. Things, however, take a sideways turn and the couples must unite and work together to protect all they hold dear.

CHAPTER 1

"*R*emember when we decided to whimsically get on the next ship and go to lands unknown?"

Violet was lying on one of the couches in her parlor. It was stifling hot and even with the lights low and the thick curtains drawn, nothing helped against the heat. Wearing her lightest dress still felt like wrapping in a wool blanket. Stockings were the bane of her existence.

Her Turkish coffee and her cocktail were on the table next to her, but she'd have to move to partake, so they were slowly moving in temperature towards each other with the coffee cooling and the ice in her cocktail melting. Only her headache had her contemplating the coffee, but she couldn't quite bring herself to put it near her mouth.

They had determined to go bathing later but Jack had a meeting, so they were waiting for him to return. A part of Vi considered abandoning her husband to dive into the pool without him, but the heat of the day would turn her skin to a burnt crisp. She needed the sun to start moving towards the horizon before she could risk diving into the water. Instead, she once again considered taking a sip from her cocktail and then rejected the idea of moving at all.

Only Denny had even appeared in the parlor that morning, and he'd explained it had been because his wife, Lila, had ordered him and his hot breath from the bedroom.

Denny glanced at Vi from his reclined position on the chaise lounge, propped up with a melting box of chocolates. "Are you referring to our most recent voyage?"

Violet held out an imperious hand for a chocolate. Denny scowled darkly, eyed the box carefully, and handed over one of his least favorites.

"You're lucky I like this one"—Violet lifted the chocolate and took a slow bite before lying back down—"given these chocolates are mine."

"They're always yours." Denny's whine was clouded by chocolate and she lifted a brow at him. It was too hot to voice a mockery. "No one loves me."

"Do you remember our trip?" Vi asked again. She sighed deeply and snuggled into her sofa. What she needed, she thought, was some sort of fan. The kind her great-grandmother would have glanced flirtingly over the top of at a man or snapped closed to make a point.

"I remember. Twins trying to murder each other's husbands, failing, and poisoning each other. It's a story I'll tell my grandchild and she won't believe me."

Violet laughed weakly, exhausted from the heat to make more of an effort. "Maybe next time we should research our ship first. Perhaps also be sure of where we're going."

"So let's never, ever do that again." Denny grunted and then demanded, "Where is everyone?"

"Jack and Ham went to meet with Smith about something

or other. I think they're working with him on a missing person."

"A child?" Denny asked and for once he didn't sound lazy. Instead he had the edge of a frantic father who suddenly cared about more than cocktails, chocolate, and afternoon naps. It was a new look for him, and he was struggling to carry it.

Consolingly, Violet replied quickly. "No, a businessman, I think. His partners are looking for him."

"I would say that's interesting, but my guess—and I'm just wildly throwing out ideas here—is that what they're missing is money." Denny popped another chocolate into his mouth and then groaned, waving his hand in front of his face. With a whimper, he added, "It's so hot."

Violet ignored the obvious to continue. "It's possible that Jack and Ham have thought of that. They're supposedly somewhat good at this whole investigating thing."

"Jack scolded you about interfering in his new collaboration with Smith and Ham, didn't he?"

Violet scowled. "It's not like I don't have my own things to do."

Denny giggled like a schoolboy. She watched him wipe a tear away before he asked, "Did Rita get scolded as well?"

Violet sat up suddenly. That idea had not occurred to her, and she needed to know. She abandoned Denny and the parlor, leaving behind her shoes to make her way to the telephone. A quick call later and Vi returned to the parlor and tossed Denny's feet from the chaise lounge.

"Hey now," he said with a bit of a groan. The glee in his eyes, however, told her that he already knew the answer to his previous question.

Vi put her hands on her hips and scowled down at him.

He grinned at her, unrepentant. "Am I in trouble for being one of the boys or am I in trouble for being right?"

"The latter," Vi told him and then took the chocolate, found one of the covered caramels—both of their favorite—and popped it into her mouth, savoring it in retaliation.

"It's not my fault that I'm brilliant, Vi. It just happens."

"Brilliant?" She put the box of chocolates just out of his reach. He tried to appease her with a meek expression.

"Maybe I have a little bit of an idea of how some men might feel even if I would never scold in such a manner."

"Never?" Vi snorted and then gave him the chocolates again. She was too hot to stay angry for long. She frowned at her cooled coffee and watered-down cocktail. "My brother staying home with his sick wife and sick daughters really make this whole cocktail situation unacceptable."

"It's not that hard to make a cocktail, Vi."

"There's an art. Don't make me kill you off in my next book. Maybe there will be werewolves or pirates. Either way —" She slowly drew her finger across her neck.

Denny laughed heartily at her threat. "Would it be bloody?"

"The grisliest scene I had ever written." Vi's solemn reply had him laughing again. "Knives, axes, fires, beetles." When she reached beetles, she petered out and repeated, "Fires."

"What about pirates and werewolves?" Denny asked seriously around another chocolate. "If I have to die, I should think it would be best to be murdered in a fight between them both. Nearly victorious, but not quite."

Vi choked on a laugh first, but then an idea occurred to her and she leaned in, almost whispering, "Can you imagine Victor's face when he read the draft? Our villain Denny on the deck of the werewolf pirate ship?"

Denny slowly sat up, his eagerness dampened only by the heat.

"Your twin would understand what you were doing immediately," Denny warned Vi.

"That doesn't mean he wouldn't revel in it." She crossed to the melting ice block on the drinks table and dipped her kerchief in the drip pan before wrapping it around her neck.

The story idea had excellent merit, especially because if she wasn't mistaken, her twin was struggling with his own series of grey days, which had almost exclusively been her purview over their life. His very occasional bouts were worse for all of them because they were so rare.

"Reveling is the winning phase of a prank," Denny said with a nod. "If you can get him to revel at our brilliance, then we've won."

"We've?" Vi asked silkily. "And who said this was a prank?"

He ignored her question without meeting her gaze. "Anything with both werewolves and pirates needs a princess."

"Oh! A pirate princess!"

"A pirate princess who falls in love with a werewolf," Denny crowed.

Vi raised a hand in the air and said, "Anything this ridiculous calls for cocktails."

She tried a woebegone face and Denny rose to mix them, groaning the whole way as though he were an old man who struggled with pain even walking across the floor.

Vi grabbed paper from the drawer and started making notes. The two of them shot ideas back and forth until Rita arrived. She threw herself onto one of the large chairs, grabbed an empty cocktail glass and begged, "Please sir, I want some more."

Her large blue eyes were as wide as a puppy's as she begged Denny to be the one to break ice off the block. She fluttered thick black lashes and then glanced at Vi out of the corner of her eye. She smirked when Denny complied with her pleading.

Rita was an arresting level of lovely. She could walk across the room and eyes would follow wherever she went. With golden hair bobbed and marcelled into waves, she was smooth and perfect. Her big blue eyes were vibrant and sparkling. They were so utterly feminine and she was so dryly witty, it was rare for many to realize just how clever her perfect gaze was. She was curvy, dressed in a light linen blue dress that emphasized her coloring, showing herself as the epitome of the bright young thing.

Violet might well have been jealous of Rita for her looks. Vi was pretty enough. With sharp features and dark hair and eyes, she was taller than average for a woman and quite slender. She was not, however, someone that would turn all heads. Vi didn't care in the least. Jack loved her and that was all she needed.

Rita had joined Vi in more than a few of the investigations that so agitated their beloveds. Ham was no happier with it than Jack. "Do you think they agreed to lecture us?" Rita asked. "I mean, they talked about it over a glass of port?"

Vi imitated Ham. "'You talk to Vi, be firm.'"

Vi's impression of her husband made Rita laugh. Her pretty blue eyes flashed with humor until Denny joined in and then they flashed with irritation.

"Yes," Denny answered Rita, ignoring her dark look. "Certainly they agreed."

He gave Rita a cocktail made with gin, orange juice, and Victor's blackberry cordial.

Rita sighed into her cup. "I can't imagine Jack as easily."

"It would have been well-intentioned," Vi muttered. "'We don't have the Yard behind us now, Ham,'" she imitated. "'If the girls get involved, they could get even more hurt than they have already been.'"

"Then they recapped all the times we've been hurt," Rita said, seeming to see the scene herself. "Me, after I came home with Martha."

"Vi and Kate," Denny added helpfully, "that terrible Christmas visit to my home."

"Not terrible. Not when we got Kate," Vi countered.

"Poor sap," Denny said, referring to Vi's brother who had met and fallen in love with Kate during that visit. "Besotted in love. Takes us all eventually, I suppose."

Violet rolled her eyes, shaking off the old injuries. Had she gotten into trouble a few times while delving into Jack's cases? Perhaps, yes, it was possible.

"It's not that the boys are right," Vi began with a mischievous expression as she held her glass against her forehead. The chill provided such a beautiful respite that she sagged into her seat with a deep sigh.

"Although they are," Denny said and then grabbed the chocolates and fled Vi's parlor before Rita and Violet could throw something more than a pillow at him.

"It's that they're right," Rita finished. She said it without restraint, given they no longer had an audience. "It does bother me though. Jack was hurt a few times. Ham has scars that he changes the story behind them time after time. We are all fragile."

"How are things at home?"

Rita paused long enough that it was evident that something was bothering her friend.

CHAPTER 2

"Father came by."

Vi waited. Rita's pause had been too long and Vi's gaze widened with mirth. She rose and refilled their drinks, slamming the ice pick down into the block until she had enough chunks to make new, cool drinks. "That's rather satisfying."

"Is it?"

"Given your tone—" Vi handed Rita a new cocktail and then slipped into the chair next to her. "I'm guessing that you might benefit from the fierce use of an ice pick."

"I would benefit from the fierce use of a lot of things. I might have even placed a pillow over my face and shrieked today after Father left."

"Oh?" Vi waited but Rita was so busy staring into the distance that Vi finally asked, "Why did he come?"

Rita blinked rather rapidly and then her gaze met Vi's and shifted. Rita was, Vi realized, rather pale. "Those Hollands brothers from my wedding have been coming by. Father

8

wanted to let Ham know, but of course, Ham was off with Jack interfering in people's lives after putting us in pretty little cages."

"Are you and Ham fighting?"

Rita paused so long that Vi thought for certain that they were. "I—" Rita shook her head and then finished, "No. No, of course not."

Their gazes met again and this time Rita's matched Vi's humor.

"All right, I confess. Ham and I have to keep consciously and desperately from arguing. We're just both so...so..."

"Intelligent and opinionated?"

"Opinionated anyway." Rita sipped her drink and then leaned back, fanning herself with her hand. She finally met Vi's eyes. "Father had other news."

"Did he?" Vi asked when Rita let the silence linger too long again.

"Father has purchased a house near ours."

"You rather thought he was going to, didn't you? Or at least leave Scotland after the scandal and the true colors of his friends becoming apparent."

Rita nibbled at her lip and Vi was surprised to see the uncertainty on her friend's face. Rita was nothing if not the confident, outgoing personification of a bright young thing. How...why...had Rita become so uncertain? Vi guessed. "Is he going to marry that woman?"

"Mmm." Rita's gaze shifted to the side. "They married while we were gone."

Again, the silence was too long and it was filled with the suffocating weight of Rita's bottled feelings.

"Mmm," Rita said again.

"Are you too full of emotion for words?" Vi's gentle tone

made them both wince. Vi reached out a sweaty hand to her friend and squeezed Rita's.

Rita had to clear her throat to answer and her voice was shaky when she did. "He knew I would understand when I discovered she was with child."

It was Vi who was now silent as she stared at Rita. The silence was a different kind of weighty and Vi had to bite down on her bottom lip to hold in the inappropriate laugh. "Are you…isn't she…my goodness. Isn't she too old?"

"Apparently not," Rita replied with an edge of bitterness. "I'm going to be a big sister."

Again that weight. It was a combination, Vi thought, of ridiculous humor, jealousy, guilt for the jealousy, and hurt.

Violet turned her glass in her hand as she fought for how to be a good friend. "You're jealous."

Rita gasped as if wounded and then admitted, "Perhaps."

"It's all right to be jealous. I've been bitterly jealous of Isolde the whole of my life, and I adore my sister. Let alone the wart. Father is kinder and more engaged with the child he knows isn't his over Victor and I."

"He did raise him," Rita said, knowing that Violet agreed.

"Emotions aren't rational. Yours or mine. It's fine if you're jealous. It's reasonable. Human even."

"I expect better of myself."

"So do I," Vi added. "I love that wart of ours. I miss him when I don't see him. I envy him his relationship with my father."

"I…thank you." Rita drained her glass.

"You need a distraction." Whenever she said anything quite so mischievously it was evident she intended to dive into the type of hijinks that would send her stepmother into spasms.

Rita smiled slowly. "A party?"

"Something ridiculous. More ridiculous than going on a voyage without any investigation."

"The opposite of my perfect wedding. From one extreme to the other," Rita said. "Prizes like Father had, but of the most ridiculous nature."

"Roller-skates," Vi suggested. "A live band. Someone serving ice cream. A party that doesn't start until most of the countryside has gone to bed."

"Your bathing pool," Rita added. "Midnight swims with candlelight."

Vi's eyes narrowed, recognizing the clever push of the party to Vi's house rather than to Rita's. Rita grinned widely and Vi said, "Fine. But you have to find the band and decide upon what we serve."

"Agreed." Rita rubbed her hands together and then groaned. "Oh, it's hot. Maybe too hot?"

Vi shook her head. "We could have a party whenever, couldn't we? Let's start it at midnight."

"I'm tired already," Rita joked, but she had slipped a piece of paper from Vi and started to make a list. "Perhaps a shade earlier. Aren't your supply of roller-skates in London? Shall we dart up and go shopping while we're there?"

"Yes," Vi said, "but in an auto. I would rather wear rags than get on a train in this heat."

"Agreed," Rita said. "Tomorrow we'll go. Will Kate come?"

"Victor said she is refusing to even dress and spending much of her time in a cool bath regretting being with child during the summer. She has made him swear they will never have another child if this one is a boy."

"Did he say yes?"

Vi rolled her eyes in reply.

Rita snorted. "Yes, of course, I forgot. He'll do whatever she wants."

"He'd have been happy with Agatha and Vivi anyway," Vi replied. "Two girls, twins, so he can lead them down the path of all the terrible things he and I did? He'd never have wanted anything else."

"Ahhh," Rita said and then grinned. "Are you and Jack?"

She drew out the question and waggled her brows to indicate she wondered whether Vi and Jack were thinking of adding to their family.

Vi leaned back and eyed her friend. From her experience that question tended to be timed in direct association with someone else reproducing. She considered for a moment, fanned herself and asked, "Going to try in the future—when the time is right—so I'm not dying of heat in the summer like Kate."

"The future, huh?" Rita's smile was sly. When Vi didn't react, Rita offered, "Ham is older than Jack."

Vi paused. "He is older than Jack. That's true." Vi waited expectantly. Was it possible? Were Rita and Ham going to have a baby, too? She lifted her brows in question.

"Yes," Rita answered. "A baby and all that."

"Yes?" Vi squealed. She hugged Rita and then let her go immediately due to the heat.

"Yes," Rita repeated. "I'm hoping for a solitary boy."

"But all the girls," Vi moaned, thinking a boy would be sad to be left out if they didn't find ways to play together.

"I know," Rita countered. "All of those options for him to fall in love with."

Vi laughed. "He's not even here, and you're already marrying him off."

"Well, Hamilton Barnes Jr. wouldn't crush his mother and

aunts by not deciding which of those daughters amongst us are the cleverest and funniest and then begging that girl to love him desperately."

Vi lifted her brows and whispered, "You've just made the suggestion that one of them is the best. Those are fighting words, my friend."

"I know," she said with wicked humor. "It'll be like Paris, the golden apple, and the goddesses."

"It'll be war," Vi agreed.

"But first," Rita countered, "it'll be a party."

Vi's devilish grin made an appearance and then they started making a list of things they'd need to get in London.

"LONDON?" Jack asked. He did it with the air of a man who was going to rearrange his schedule to dart up to the city with her even though she only wanted to get a few things from the London house, hire a fellow to serve ice cream at their party, and get a new party dress.

She also wanted to go to London to avoid the desire to meddle in whatever he was up to. The truth of the matter was that she'd start the new book—or perhaps a novella—to tease Victor, but that would hardly occupy her mind full-time.

What was she going to do next? Bother Jack? Plant roses? Redecorate another room? All of those things sounded terribly boring. Victor was occupied to an extent that Vi had to admit made her quite jealous. She had every intention of going over and bothering him often and knew he'd welcome her presence, but still—still, it was rather unsatisfactory, wasn't it?

"London." Vi pressed her hands to either of his cheeks, careful to keep their bodies separated due to the ridiculous heat, but she squished his face and told him, "Rita and I. A girls' trip."

Jack's gaze narrowed and she could almost see the calculation in his head of whether he even thought that he wanted to disagree. Let alone disagree and argue.

"I am a grown woman, Jack," she reminded him.

"And so very capable," he agreed. "I think I've a bit of a nervous old aunt in me when it comes to you, Vi."

"I'll be fine," she told him again, patting his cheek lightly. "The great risk will be that the heat melts me into nothing. My goodness, Jack." She eyed him, knowing Rita was expecting and wondering if he knew and what he felt. "We might need to sail to the North Pole."

"A bit of an overreaction, wouldn't you say?"

"I would say no such thing, sirrah," she told him with a laugh. "Time for my third cold bath of the day."

Instead of bathing, however, they returned to the Roman-style swimming pool they'd added to the property and swam in the moonlight. The coolness of the water was such a relief that Vi didn't even mind when Jack moved closer, or when the heat of the evening shifted into something else entirely.

CHAPTER 3

The auto windows were down, they were both wearing wet kerchiefs around their necks, and they had been wise enough to bring thermoses full of iced coffee, iced lemonade, and iced champagne. Even with the air blowing in from the opened windows, the car felt like an oven.

Vi groaned, "They're going to find this auto on the side of the road with only two puddles left as evidence that we ever existed."

Rita huffed as though she would have laughed but it was too hot to do so. They carried on the drive despite the heat and the creeping desire to turn back. By the time they stopped for lunch, they were out of the coffee and the lemonade.

Vi wanted nothing more than a vat of something cool, a refreshed wet kerchief, and a cool breeze. The only breeze they could get, however, was a hot one that felt as though the underworld was being aired out onto England.

"Do we have to get out?" Rita sighed and the friends eyed each other.

"I am regretting being independent," Vi confessed. "Why did I care that Jack lectured me?"

"I am regretting leaving your poolside. Why didn't we send a servant up to London to get what we wanted? We could have given them some sort of heat bonus."

Vi's answer was to prop her head against her hands gripping the steering wheel. "I dream of a world with ice buckets in the auto and with the movement of the air from the driving. What do you think? Would it work?"

Rita shook her head and rolled her eyes at the same time.

"There must be some way to cool an automobile on a hot day."

"Sailing is the answer."

"Time for a sailboat then, my friend. Something big enough for all of us. We can take a ship to somewhere cooler should it ever get this hot again."

Rita's expression said the idea of a yacht had merit.

"I'm too hot to eat," Vi said, "but I need something more to drink."

They finally went inside and the switch from blazing sun to thick walls and high ceilings was enough for both of them to collapse in the chairs of a table in the corner. In a moment, they had re-wet their kerchiefs, wound them around their necks, and ordered fruit and gazpacho.

"What do we do, do you think?" Rita stared towards the exit, and both of them had been watching other fools come into the restaurant, collapse as dramatically as Vi and Rita, and then laugh to themselves. Was the whole of the world full of fools who left their houses during the heat when they didn't have to?

Vi sipped her cooled ginger beer and wondered why hadn't she and Rita decided to take a trip to the seaside instead? "Do you mean should we take a room or shall we carry on?"

Rita snorted. "Can you imagine if we didn't appear in London and then the boys realized we hadn't arrived? Heads would roll, and they'd be ours."

Vi grinned and said, "It's half-tempting."

"Jack would lose his mind," Rita said with a laugh. She sipped her own drink before she added, "As would Ham, of course." She paused and then added almost wistfully, "I bet they've got quite clean sheets here."

The restaurant had an inn overhead and that was all one could wish. Excellent food, thick walls, so clean it nearly gleamed despite the dimmed lights due to the heat. The desire to stay was compelling, especially because they didn't have to go to London and they could come or go as they pleased.

"I couldn't worry Jack. We'd either have to stay here, go home, or go to London, but if we stay here, a telephone call to our lads is a must."

"I don't like to admit that this is all a stupid stunt." Rita's expression turned sour, and she eyed Violet, silently demanding a confession of her own.

Vi wondered if her feminine stubbornness would agree. It did, immediately, and she had to roll her eyes at herself. Jack, Victor, Ham, and Denny were the best of modern men. They saw the women in their lives as intelligent and capable creatures. The only time they went a little feudal lord-ish was when their loved ones were in danger. It was fair of them, both Vi and Rita knew; they were physically weaker than men. You could be as smart, as capable as anything, but you couldn't deny that—in most cases—a woman wasn't as phys-ically strong as a man.

"A stupid stunt?" Vi snorted and then grinned wickedly. "The reality of the matter is that I won't be returning home without proving the point that has no need of proving. Making both me and you the most ridiculous of women."

"Ham did laugh at me when I packed my bag in a huff and told him it was his fault for ordering me off of his business."

"As though they aren't utterly right in asking us to keep out when we expect the same."

Rita stared at Vi and then started giggling. "I might not torture Ham this way," Rita started suddenly, "but I could do it to my father."

"Your father-the-fertile?" Vi asked with a devilish smirk.

"Papa the great sower of seed." Rita paused and then gagged. "Not something I want to think about."

"He's not going to stop loving you," Violet told her gently when she looked up and saw that Rita was sad.

"I'm not just jealous of the baby," Rita told Vi. "I'm jealous of Father's new wife, his stepdaughter, and the fact that he seems more involved with them than he ever was with me. I am filled with jealousy on all sides. Like a venomous plant bursting with the need to spray my poison."

Vi choked on a laugh at the look on Rita's face. Carefully, when Vi had her humor in control, she said, "Maybe he's realized that the time you have together slips by so quickly. Perhaps he feels as though he's gotten a second chance with the new women in his life, and he doesn't want to make the same mistakes."

"Maybe," Rita sighed, flinching at the memory, "having two wives murdered has shown him that life is fragile."

"He dumped all that money on your wedding and your

house because he's trying to show he loves you," Violet told her friend. She patted her arm. "And a treasure hunt? One doesn't come up with some ridiculous prize and have a multi-day event as though you were a princess if he didn't adore you beyond words."

Rita laughed lightly and muttered mulishly, despite the light of humor in her eyes, "Perhaps."

Vi's head tilted and she asked suddenly, "Whatever happened to the prize from the search? Did your father give it to the second-in-place?"

"Indeed not. Those Hollands brothers demanded the prize and Father doesn't like to be commanded."

"Demanded?"

"They said they won since Reese Stafford died."

"Therefore?" Vi asked.

"It's still in the parlor of our house, a bloody reminder. A dented, bejeweled, gaudy goblet. It's ridiculous."

"What did the Hollands brothers do?"

"Objected strenuously and furiously, but you aren't a businessman like Father was without being rather used to people upset with you. I think he might have laughed and asked the fellow for a copy of his contract."

"Oh," Vi winced.

"Ham ensured those who came in second and third place got secondary prizes and Father was furious about that too."

"Such a wonderful event," Vi said dryly. She caught the attention of the waitress and begged to get their thermoses refilled with anything that would be cold and see them through to London. At the same time, they refreshed the wet kerchiefs around their necks once again.

The moment they stepped out onto the little country village street, Vi winced. The skies were perfectly blue, without a cloud to provide even a shred of cover. The sun was high and so strong, it seemed angry. There was a sheen of heat in the air around the moving automobiles.

Rita sighed, then went to hook her arm through Vi's and shook her head. "No, too hot. Well, regardless," Rita opened the door of the auto and then groaned. "Onward, darling. Onward and forward."

Vi took the driver's seat and headed down the road. They both sighed in relief to leave the village with its stifling buildings behind. A copse of woods was just ahead and they considered stopping and napping under the trees and carrying on in the cool of the evening, but the weight of Jack's and Ham's worries kept them going.

They reached London and found their way to Vi's house. The usual servants were at the country house, but Vi's business manager and friend, Beatrice, lived in the city house full-time. They also kept at least one servant on the premises to look after things.

When Vi arrived, she let herself in and then crossed to the parlor, throwing herself on the Chesterfield with a sigh.

"What now?" Rita asked.

"Baths," Vi declared.

"Dinner out?"

Vi shook her head against the seat of the couch. No one was present to cook and neither of them were reasonable cooks, but Vi figured they were likely enough to have eggs and bread in the house, and she could manage toast and an omelet. "It's too hot."

Vi eventually dragged herself up the stairs to bath and put on her coolest sleeping wear covered by a light kimono. She wandered across the hall and knocked on Rita's door. "Rita darling, are you feeling all right?"

"I'm fine," Rita called. "Are you being solicitous because I'm a breeder now? Or is it the heat?"

"Both." Vi laughed. "Your poor child. Over-protective father on one side and a mad mother on the other."

"Let alone the crazy Aunt Vi," Rita countered. "What are the chances we'll find something frozen and delectable in the kitchen?"

CHAPTER 4

"*L*ow," Beatrice said from the open doorway. She grinned widely at the two women. "Hello. So glad you made it safely. There's a fellow here who wants to see you. He's come time and again."

Vi squealed and spun, hugging Beatrice. About the visitor, Vi said, "I'm still covered in sweat and dust from the road, and we are not at home. Tell whoever dared to show up at our house almost the moment we arrived to go away. Channel my stepmother if necessary. Be imperious and dismissive. My heavens."

"What if it is your father who sent the fellow?" Rita asked quizzically as Beatrice nodded without surprise.

"It isn't," Vi told Rita. "He doesn't keep a lookout for me, and I certainly didn't tell him I was coming."

"Gerald?" Rita asked, referring to Vi's oldest brother. "Or Tomas?" Vi's brother-in-law was one of Vi's long-time friends, and she had been closer to him than anyone other than Victor for years. She loved them both but neither were at the door.

"Is the visitor a member of my family?" Vi asked to stop Rita's teasing.

"No," Beatrice replied with a laugh.

"Then, make him go away, please, dear one."

Beatrice assured she would while Vi finally escaped to the bath to wash her face and rinse off. When she returned to her bedroom swathed in a kimono, she found Rita had done the same and Beatrice had brought up chilled coffee and cucumber sandwiches.

"You don't have to wait on us," Vi said, but she took the coffee gratefully and sank into a chair in her boudoir. She and Jack shared the master bedroom, so they turned the very Victorian mistress-of-the-house bedroom into Vi's private space. The dragons on her armoire, the typing table and covered typewriter, the photograph of her mother and great-aunt all proclaimed this room fully Vi's.

"Did you confess?" Vi demanded.

Neither Beatrice nor Rita appeared sure if Vi was speaking of themselves, so Vi grinned and expanded on her comment. "Both of you have been up to no good, I can see." To Beatrice Vi said, "Rita's going to be a mother and a sister."

Beatrice's mouth dropped opened just as Vi was struck with a pillow from behind.

Vi tossed the pillow back at Rita but her aim was off. She blamed it on the heat. "Now," she said to Beatrice, "what have you done?"

Beatrice blushed brightly, but she said nothing.

"Something," Rita mused. When Beatrice didn't disclose her secret, Rita told Vi, "She'll confide in us eventually." She sighed as the heat hit her and she attempted to fan herself with her hand. "Do you think Smith could be sent for ices?"

"Smith?" Beatrice asked and then laughed.

"Smith?" Vi demanded with a snort. "Not Smith. Have you gone mad? We left him in the country with our husbands."

Beatrice's love was a private investigator as well as a man who seemed to have no morals and no mercy. "He's in Edinburgh," Beatrice told them with a frown.

"Edinburgh? I thought he was working a case with Jack and Ham," Rita said, brow crinkling as she tossed her pillow back to the bed. "Perhaps I have gone mad. The heat is just so sweltering."

"Smith is following a lead to find that man who absconded with company funds."

Vi lifted a brow and then fanned herself. "So we're on our own for ices?"

Beatrice rolled her eyes. "No. Jemmy is here looking after the house. I'll send him and tell him he can have one too. He'll be thrilled."

"Ooh, then send him for those spicy Chinese noodles," Rita begged.

Vi shook her head and told Beatrice, "Here we go again with another round of food madness. Of course she wants the noodles that make you feel as though you're on fire, it's as hot as Hades outside. If we didn't know she was expecting, we'd know it now."

"I do feel like I tripped right into the nether realm," Rita said. "It's hot here, Bea. Why don't you come with us back to the country house? We're having a ridiculous party. All of the oddest things we can think of that, when put together, create fun and frivolity."

"Yes," Vi said instantly, "I insist. You can wait until the heat wave is over to come back to London. Especially with Smith gone. It must be lonely here."

Beatrice was shaking her head but Vi groaned and said, "There's nothing truly needing your attention, is there?"

Beatrice paused long enough that Vi could see the answer was no but that Beatrice felt guilty for leaving. "Surely anything could wait?"

Beatrice hesitated and Rita added, "Vi could use the help with her party."

"That's what we pay the others for," Vi said. "We want you there, Beatrice. Besides, will Smith return to the country where Jack and Ham are working?"

Beatrice nodded and it was amusing how the mention of where Smith would be going was enough to quash her resistance. The unspoken teasing was wrapped around Smith, which caused Beatrice to blush deeply, but she finally relented. "All right."

In mercy, Vi told Beatrice, "Bring your bathing suit."

"Oh, and a party dress," Rita added. "We'll be having a midnight, roller-skating, trying Victor's new line of spirits, ice cream, lobster-something party."

"That's a long name," Beatrice said dryly. "I don't know if it'll fit on the invitations."

Vi snorted. She drew out the paper with the lists that she and Rita had made. "We need to move quickly. I think London is maybe a full thousand degrees hotter than the country. We've got to send the invites out while we're here and then gather up what we can."

"We'll need something to wear the morning after the party when nearly everyone is still around." Rita added to the list, leaning over Vi's shoulder to make sure that it was written down. "Maybe more roller-skates."

Vi nodded and added to the list as the other two called out ideas. When they had finished, Vi asked, "Who was the fellow so rudely demanding me?"

"Hollands," Beatrice answered with a look of frustration. "He wasn't here for you, Vi, but Rita, but you seemed united in turning him away, and honestly, he's come so many times, I rather delighted in it. He's been a right nuisance."

"Which one?" Rita asked with a frown. "And seek me here?"

"Mostly Edward, sometimes the doctor. Because you were gone from your home in the country, and you don't have a London house. Those brothers knew you'd be here if you came back, and your father told him that he didn't want to see him around again."

"About the goblet?" Vi guessed. "He is determined, isn't he? Why does he care so much?"

Beatrice shook her head with the air of a woman who did not care in the least why, though it was also evident that she very much wanted the man to stop coming by. "After the last visit, I swore on my mother's grave that I'd warn you as soon as I saw you, but they must have been watching the house."

"That's just disturbing," Rita muttered.

"Feels like what happened to Kate," Vi repeated. "Or poor Harriet."

"Or you," Beatrice added. "Bates didn't just stalk Simone Reeves, he stalked you, Vi."

Vi shuddered, and then she pushed the memory away. "Ices. Roller-skates. But ancient goblets? Anything else, please. I won't be able to sleep if we talk about what happened and Jack isn't here to make me feel safe."

"Well, your bedroom isn't that comfortable for all of us, and it is coolest in the library," Beatrice suggested and Vi nodded immediately. They followed Beatrice down the stairs carrying the cucumber sandwiches and cooled coffee.

"Isn't your mother alive?" Rita asked Beatrice a moment after they settled themselves. "I could have sworn that Hargreaves said he was visiting her while we were on that terrible journey to Norway."

"She's alive. I swore to tell you on Mother's grave, so it would be believable," Beatrice agreed with a grin. "Hollands, however, didn't know that, and he really was being most pressing. He kept demanding your address, and I could hardly comply simply because he was insistent. Some other man came by several times after that, never leaving his name and never arriving when Smith was here. He wanted to talk to you too. I think Edward Hollands must have found himself someone else to come by and bother me."

Rita frowned with a deep forehead crease. "That doesn't sound like Hollands. I mean...he wasn't my favorite friend, but he is a friend."

"He didn't come across like one," Beatrice told Rita flatly. "Are you so sure?"

"Oh, I don't know. I suppose I wouldn't be terribly surprised if he did something that I didn't love, but I don't think I'd be afraid of him."

Beatrice shrugged. It was clear that the Hollands brothers had made an enemy of Vi's one-time maid, one-time secretary, and current friend and business manager. Regarding the matter, Vi found that she trusted Beatrice's opinion over Rita. Not because Vi didn't think well of Rita's judgement, but because Rita had always been the beautiful heiress who people did whatever was necessary to be around. How a man treated a random woman, his mother, and a woman in a position of lesser power was far more telling than how he treated the wealthiest woman he knew.

Beatrice crossed to the library door. "I'll just send Jemmy off for noodles and ices, shall I?"

Vi nodded and followed after, digging through the kitchen ice box for cocktails mixings, promising Beatrice something cold, and then Vi brought the ice bucket back to the library. "Did you want something to drink, Rita?"

"It has been giving me headaches," Rita muttered. "It's quite hard to be me right now. What with the protective, loving husband, the child on the way, and the future sibling."

Vi looked up from the bar they'd installed in the library and lifted a brow. Rita was laid full out on one of the sofas, fanning herself with a piece of paper. Her ankles were crossed, and she wasn't pretending at anything other than an evening at home with a nightgown and no shoes. Let alone those torture devices that stockings had become.

"This is cozy," Vi said. "I could use some coziness in my life after that boat trip. Something like an afternoon tea with a vicar, strawberry scones, and peacefully drifting in a rowboat."

Rita laughed so hard she cried and then admitted, "I miss Ham, and I'm an idiot."

"You haven't even been gone a day," Vi mocked as though she wasn't already thinking that bringing up Preston Bates had ruined any chance she had for sleep without Jack.

"But my bed will be lonely without him."

"It's too hot to snuggle," Vi suggested, but she knew she'd rather sleep safely in Jack's warm arms than coolly without him. The truth for Vi was that she'd probably be unable to sleep and spend half the night sitting in front of her typewriter working on that piece of madness she and Denny had concocted.

Then, because life liked to make a mockery of Vi, she'd wake with a headache. She'd be in a foul mood due to the lack of sleep, her own lack of stalwartness, and then buy whatever dress would 'do' and then have the auto filled with petrol. That way, she could return to Jack—who she had only left to make some sort of idiotic point that was so irrational he hadn't argued with her.

By the time they'd lingered over their noodles and ices, sipped their drinks, and split the list of things to do the next day, Vi was already planning on giving up sleep to work on her draft. The only agreement was that they'd all focus on getting their part of the lists completed as quickly as possible so they could leave the hellfire of London for the cooler countryside.

None of them had to say aloud they were hurrying home to their loves and not to escape the heat. They all knew the truth, and they all wanted to be home. Jack. Ham. Smith. Home.

CHAPTER 5

After visiting the dress shop together the moment they opened, the three friends took their lists, separate cabs, and attacked London with their goals. Vi's list included dropping by her brother Gerald's home to invite him and send him after her cousin, Algie.

"Talked to a fellow about you at the club today," Gerald said with the slow idleness that didn't seem to understand that Vi was in a rush.

He was a man, Vi thought, who had rarely been in a hurry at all. He reminded her of her father, only much younger. Gerald had the casual arrogance of a man who didn't even realize he shed pride like a snake shed its skin.

"Did you tell him that I was a joy to the world? Actually valuable above rubies? Did you say that you were blessed beyond measure that I called you brother?"

Gerald didn't get her jokes as well as Jack and Victor so her oldest brother stared at Vi as though she'd lost her mind.

"The heat," she said in casual explanation.

He lifted a brow and then glanced at the parlor. "Come sit. Smythe will bring something cool to drink."

Vi took a seat after handing her brother the stack of invitations. "Do have Smythe mail these for me, please?" With a wicked grin, she added on the list of extra food that needed to be brought to the house. Her brother wasn't so amused, but his man took the list and the enclosed thirty pounds with a nod.

"There's swimming," Vi said, knowing her brother's flat contained nothing of the same and that he and his wife were lingering in London to avoid their stepmother, Lady Eleanor.

"Perhaps we'll ship out after your place. Your Amalfi villa?"

Vi agreed to lend the place to him and then asked, "So why were you talking about me at the club?"

"Some fellow trying to find your friend."

"Hollands?" Vi asked in extreme surprise.

"He was with a crackpot gent I know. Always chasing treasure, ruins, theories, and myths. He's the laughingstock of the club, but his father is a marquis."

"I'm curious as to why I care about this fellow other than he is obsessed with a prize from Rita's wedding."

"It's not that, Vi. They think it's the start of an ancient scavenger hunt."

"What are you talking about?" Vi demanded with a raised brow. "Don't be ridiculous."

"It's not me," Gerald told her idly. "It's them. They're trying to quietly drum up money to finance their treasure hunt."

Vi had to blink rather rapidly as she attempted to understand what her brother was telling her. "They want to hunt an ancient treasure using the goblet?"

"They call it Nemo's Goblet."

"Nemo?" Vi's head tilted as she stared at her brother. She accepted the cold ginger beer from Smythe as she asked, "Nemo as in nobody? Or Nemo as in the fiction?"

"I have no idea." Gerald grinned at her and said, "I gave them money."

"You did?"

"Or promised it."

"Why?" Vi demanded.

"It was an if-then situation."

Vi's gaze narrowed on the self-satisfied expression on her brother's face. "The if being—"

"That they get Rita to give them permission to search on her property."

Vi's mouth dropped as her brother started chuckling like a child. "You encouraged them."

"I suggested they be quite dogged. Told them both you and Rita were impressed and energized by perseverance in the face of opposition. Especially when no one believed in the mission, nay—calling, of the sufferer."

"Did you use the word sufferer?" Vi asked, still gaping. She knew her expression was giving her oldest brother nothing but delight.

"Oh, I used it. I also suggested he focus his efforts on you. Said you were the leader of your merry band of fools."

"I'm telling Jack." She hated that she said it the moment it exited her mouth.

"Jack will think it's as funny as I do."

"Perhaps," Vi agreed. "Until he has to deal with the dogged perseverer."

That only made Gerald laugh harder.

"Since when am I the target of your pranks?"

"It was just too easy."

Vi frowned at him and then said, "You're getting the worst of the guest rooms."

"I'll still be using your bathing pool."

Vi couldn't help but grin at the look on his face. "You're a fiend."

"You love it."

"It was a good one." Vi rose and crossed to him, lightly kicking him in the shin and then dropping a kiss on his face. "I've got to get the rest of my list done."

"I thought Smythe was doing your list."

"Only the things I can pawn off on him."

"Fine then, go. Lottie and I will be there the day before your party, so we can recover from the journey."

"I'VE GOT IT ALL. We can go home soon!" Vi crowed as she entered the house, pretending she hadn't dumped half of her list on Smythe. She was going to keep that bit to herself. She didn't think either of her friends had returned yet, but victory needed to be announced even to an empty house.

The afternoon had given her an idea of what it might be like to be a pie in the oven. There seemed to be no breeze at all in the whole of London, and with the feel of bodies pressing in on each other, the sun burning down upon them, and the stifling exhaust of vehicles, it was just all the worse. As a people, they radiated more and more heat.

She frowned as she entered the slightly cooler library to find both of her friends fanning themselves with new fans, each holding a chilled drink, and each without shoes.

"So you've finished?" Rita asked idly. "We can leave? I'm more than ready."

Vi's gaze narrowed and she muttered, "The earliest that some things can be delivered is tomorrow morning. We're stuck until at least noon." If it didn't involve her also being stuck in London, she would have grinned at Rita's long, suffering sigh.

"We'll have another long hot drive," Rita replied. Her eyes were closed, her cheeks were flushed, and glistening would be the kind description. The reality was both Rita and Beatrice looked as if they'd been dunked in a tank, and Vi was sure she wasn't much better. "I want to go home as soon as possible. I might have cried this morning when I woke up and Ham's side of the bed was smooth and perfect."

"You cried," Vi told Rita, "because you are with child and a little mad."

"A little might be too generous," Beatrice said with a wink at Vi, who had kicked off her shoes and was making herself a drink. The ice bucket was mostly full of melted water with a few chunks, but she fished out what she could, filling her glass and then using a small chunk on her arms and neck.

She crossed to her friends and laughed at the look on Rita's face. Her expression said she both knew she'd gone mad and hated the fact. The moment Vi was seated, Rita threw a fan her way.

"Let's have dinner out," Vi suggested, unfolding the fan. "We'll go to the Savoy or somewhere else delicious and have drinks and food placed in front of us and perhaps even run into people we know. It'll be the best way to spend an evening that is this hot." She waved the fan back and forth and closed her eyes with the slight breeze. "If this heat wave isn't over by the time our party is finished and we all survive to that date," Vi said, "we'll have to go to the villa and wait until someone writes to us that we're back to regular temperatures in England. Gerald is planning the same, but I have little compunction about ruining a romantic trip for him. You won't believe what he's done."

Vi told Beatrice and Rita about the Hollands brothers, her brother's interference, and the idea of some sort of historic mystery.

"How ridiculous," Beatrice said over the sound of three frantically moving fans.

Rita's eyes brightened and she said, "How…fun."

Vi lifted a brow.

"It feels a bit like there's a division between us and the boys." Rita's tone was innocent but her gaze was not.

"Because they asked us to stay out of their work?"

Beatrice snorted and both Rita and Vi looked her way. Beatrice tried for an innocent look of her own and when it didn't work, she said, "I wish Smith would leave me out of his cases."

Rita and Vi stared at each other and then slowly turned to stare at Beatrice. She went from a puppy-like innocence to a blushing guilt.

"What does he want you to do?"

The blush deepened.

With a slow and dramatic question, Vi asked, "Exactly what have you done?"

Beatrice leapt to her feet. "If we want to eat at one of the nicer places, we'll need to make a reservation."

She left the library for the office phone and Rita's laughter chased Beatrice from the room.

"What do you think she's done?" Rita asked Vi.

"With Smith—" Vi paused as she considered an array of possibilities. "Anything."

Vi left the library herself and headed for her bathroom. It was hotter up the stairs, but her bath would let her chill in the water and that value couldn't be overestimated. She left the bath only when her fingers had wrinkled and her body temperature had dropped to the point where she had chills.

She pulled herself from the water and the heat hit her immediately. Vi examined her closet with a scowl on her face. Every article of clothing looked too hot. She didn't want to wear any of it. She flipped through her dresses with a speed that rejected anything with sleeves or length. She finally settled on a wine-red dress that had only straps on the shoulders, a deep dip near her chest, and a skirt made mostly of fringe. She stared at her stockings for a long time before she gave them her darkest look and put them on. She chose a pair of shoes and then rushed down the stairs where it was mildly cooler.

"They had better serve something amazing at the restaurant," Vi said, using her new fan so quickly she was surprised it hadn't fallen to pieces. "I am so hot and these stockings are…just…"

"It's as if Satan designed them," Beatrice muttered. "As if he rose up from the depths and thought, what can I do to make women miserable? Stockings and a heat wave."

"Oh," Rita said, "I'll never think of them anyway else now. Underthings created by the torturer of mankind. However, Vi, they have shrimp cocktails, oysters, salmon mousse, and a divine lemon cake."

"As long as it's chilled," Vi said, knowing she was being grumpy. "I'm sorry I'm a beast. I am so hot. I have never been happier that we put in that swimming pool, and I am furious it's hours away with Jack, who is probably swimming right now, happy as a...a...I don't know. It's too hot to be clever. He's happy as a happy man."

"Ah," Rita teased, "she's missing her husband."

"She didn't sleep last night," Beatrice told Rita, daring to tease for one of the first times since transitioning from servant to beloved friend. "She never does when Jack isn't there. Did you write?"

"She did," Rita groaned. "I didn't sleep well either and then that tap, tap, tap. It was maddening."

Beatrice leaned forward to whisper, "Then it stops just long enough for you to start to sleep—"

"Only the typing starts again the very moment you start to slip into sleep."

"Leave me alone," Vi said lamely and then they left for the black cab.

CHAPTER 6

"We're weak women these days," Rita announced as she caught Vi yawning in the black cab, "unable to sleep without our loves."

Vi didn't see any reason to argue. Jack had become as integral to her as breathing, and she didn't think it was weak to admit she was in love. She was in love and was grateful to be so. Rita was desperately gone for Ham. Even when Rita had half-hated Ham, she'd loved him. Beatrice was also just as in love, if Vi read the signs right.

In fact—Vi's head tilted. Wasn't that interesting? Beatrice was blushing deeply and staring out the window of the auto.

Vi couldn't help herself or the smirk that spread across her face as she leaned towards Beatrice. "Not sleeping well, Beatrice?"

The blush deepened as Rita burst into laughter. "Our Beatrice has succumbed."

"And joined us on the not sleeping side." Vi's eyes moved

over Beatrice's blushing face. "Ahhhh, you're in love, Beatrice. With Smith."

"Is that so hard to believe?" Beatrice asked defensively. Her gaze moved anywhere but meeting Vi and Rita's eyes. Beatrice ran her finger under the edge of her neckline as if it were too tight. "I—"

Before she could complete her thought, Vi and Rita—in unison—answered Beatrice's question. "Yes."

"But—" Beatrice met their eyes with surprise. "He's—"

"Admit it," Rita added. "Admit that Smith is a difficult man to fall in love with. I can't imagine how you did it."

Beatrice licked her lips and then said slowly, "No, not really. I slid right into it."

Vi and Rita glanced at each other and then looked their question.

Beatrice shifted slightly and said, "He's a bit overwhelming for a lot of people."

Vi nodded. Her eyes were fixed on Beatrice even as the fan fluttered hard and the darkness of the evening was punctuated by occasional flashes of lights from the street lamps.

"So—" Beatrice cleared her throat and shifted again, "when he focuses all of that wit and deviousness and—"

Rita upped the speed of her fanning and Vi glanced and then nodded. "It's—" Vi struggled for the word, but Beatrice knew what it was.

"It's intoxicating. Like the finest wine and the strongest cocktail and an excellent dessert and a sunny day after a streak of grey days. A late Christmas morning, lingering in bed. When he turns all of that on you, it's all the things that you savor."

Vi considered, shivered, and then said, "I could imagine giving in to such a thing."

"It wasn't so much giving in as trusting him," Beatrice admitted. "He's hard to trust. He's so veiled and so willing to set aside all the things that the rest of the world cares about, but when he turns all that focus on you?" She shivered. "Eventually, he made me realize that I could trust him." She lifted her brows and tilted her head, adding with stark honesty, "Even if everyone else should think twice."

"Color me smitten," Rita said with a low laugh.

"If anyone understands, it's us," Vi told Beatrice gently. "Smith is more overtly intense but Jack and Ham are cut from a similar cloth, I think." Vi paused for a long moment and then asked curiously, "So, is Smith his real name?"

Beatrice coughed on a laugh and then her face smoothed into relief when the black cab stopped outside of the restaurant.

"Oh look," Beatrice said, "we're here." And she hopped out of the automobile before the others could press her.

Rita paused long enough to ask, "Should we let her get away with that?"

"Would you share Ham's secrets if you knew them?"

Rita stilled long enough that Vi guessed Rita possessed Ham's just as Vi was aware of Jack's and Beatrice had been entrusted with Smith's.

"Fine," Rita muttered. "But I'm having two rounds of oysters and I don't want to hear anything about it."

"I wouldn't have cared regardless," Vi said as she followed Rita out of the auto.

The restaurant was well-lit with jazz music pouring from the open windows and doors. The wail of the trumpet filled the air and there was a breeze caused by passing traffic that seemed nearly arctic after the last few hours of stifling heat.

Beatrice had thought to make a reservation, so they were

greeted by a waiter within a moment. They could follow only a few steps before a man stepped forward and said, "Rita! Finally!"

He reached out and took hold of Rita's arm, and Vi noticed those grasping fingers before she moved to the man's face.

"Is everything all right, ma'am?" the maitre'd asked.

Rita twisted her arm away and smiled cheerily. "All is well. Hullo, Hollands. We've just got our table now. Perhaps I can find you after?"

"No, please. I just—"

Rita lifted a brow and the man cleared his throat and stepped back. "Sorry, sorry. Of course. Maybe you'd like to meet for drinks after dinner? My treat?"

Rita hesitated.

"Rita, we're longtime friends." Hollands put on a smile. "Come now. Give me a few minutes."

"Ma'am?" the maitre'd asked again, looking over his shoulder towards the table they'd reserved.

"Yes, yes," Beatrice said, "I'll follow you while my friend says hello." Beatrice escaped with the air of someone who was relieved to go. "I'll order drinks."

Vi glanced after Beatrice and then at Rita, who had apparently decided to confront the issue head on. "Is this about the goblet?"

"It's the Goblet of Nemo," the man said in a fervent whisper as if he were revealing a state secret.

"That sounds fake," Vi told him. He shot her a dark look, recognized her only after he'd done so, and then looked regretful.

"It's not fake. Nemo means nobody."

"Yes, I know." Vi rolled her eyes and glanced at Rita

before she turned back to Hollands. It was the elder of the brothers, and Vi couldn't quite remember his name, but she remembered that he hadn't been the one carrying the bag of poisons and nonsense. "That name isn't a likely name for a treasure that supposedly has been hidden for centuries."

"The story of where it came from isn't clear. The name Nemo was given by those who uncovered the first layer of secrets. But the ruins on your estate date back centuries," he said to Rita.

Rita turned to Vi. "Of course, they were able to find the tale of the history. They were able to find the goblet. But they weren't able to find the real name of it?"

With a furious hiss that Hollands tried and failed to hold back, he retorted. "That's why they called it the Nemo. The pages of history are obscured by idiots who threw things away that were valuable."

"And you were the one who was able to see through the obfuscation to the truth that no one else has been bright enough to recognize?"

"Please, Rita. Please."

Vi stared at her pregnant, emotional friend. Rita was mad if her heart strings played so easily under Hollands's pleading.

Rita took a deep breath in and Vi knew she had given in. "We're having a party," Rita told him. "We'll look for your treasure together."

The man's eyes widened and he grabbed Rita's hand, squeezing it too tightly. "Thank you. You'll see. You'll see, Rita. It'll be just what I said. When?"

"Saturday. You can stay at Vi's house."

Vi shot Rita a dark look, which only made her laugh.

"Saturday!" He laughed and then hugged Rita. Her arms

were sticking out from him as she avoided touching Hollands's back. "Saturday!"

He turned and fled out the building.

"How did he know we were here?" Vi asked.

Rita shrugged.

"You realize that's bothersome, right?"

"You realize you're sensitive since Preston Bates."

"Rightfully so," Vi shot back, meeting Rita's gaze stonily.

"Rightfully so," Rita agreed. "Maybe we should be careful with him until we're sure he's just a foolish man who's believed some fairy tale and not someone who will smother us in the dark in order to take credit for a mythical treasure hunt."

THE COZY TABLES in the darkened restaurant had been spread out to help with the heat, allowing the light breeze to circulate among the patrons, and though it wasn't quite cool in the restaurant, it was better than Vi had imagined.

She sighed in sheer joy when they were led towards a table in the corner next to a window. "Bless your perfect heart," Vi told Beatrice as she was seated in the corner, taking her glass of chilled champagne. They sipped their drinks and enjoyed the respite before their appetizers arrived, but then Hollands returned.

"Is it all right if I bring my brother?" he asked before being acknowledged.

Rita nodded with an exasperated air the man didn't even notice.

He added, almost apologetically, "I have an investor."

"To find treasure at my house?" Rita asked scathingly.

"We might allow you to see the goblet. We might allow you to conduct your hunt, but bringing in a slew of investors to my home? That's not something we're discussing right now."

A look of extreme distress and out and out poorly disguised frustration bordering on the edge of anger had Rita giving Hollands a challenging look. He faced off with her and then, as if understanding that she could ruin his plan only occurred to him at that moment, he struggled to put on a look of control.

"Ah," he stuttered, "yes, of course. Of course."

"What in the world?" Vi hissed to Beatrice despite the man's presence.

Beatrice's expression said she was still not surprised by Hollands.

Vi muttered, "How many times did he stop by the house?"

"So often Smith threatened him and then the man still came back."

Vi's gaze returned to the fellow and Rita. He was leaning down and talking rapidly and Rita finally lost her patience. "I've already invited you to the party this week-end," she said with a warning note in her voice. "If you want to bring it up with Ham again, at that time, you can do so."

A frustrated expression crossed his face once again, but Rita didn't slow her tirade.

"I get you want to do your little treasure hunt. I get you want to use the goblet to do so. Maybe you even feel like the goblet is owed to you. I also understand that you didn't win."

"But the winner died," Hollands shot out in a furious cough. "He died before the prizes were handed out."

"Which doesn't make you the winner," Rita snapped. "I told you that you can discuss it again with Ham. Now leave me alone or I'll remove that option as well and your invitation will be revoked."

"I am dogged in pursuit of what I know is right. I will persevere in the face of any obstacle." He intoned the words like a martyr facing death.

Vi bit down on her bottom lip but her laughter escaped regardless. Her brother was the devil, but she couldn't wait to tell him about this day.

"I didn't expect you to be like this," the man hissed at Vi and then tried again for a conciliatory look. "Rita, you know me."

"Come to the party," she said. "Now go away. It's too hot for this nonsense."

The look he gave Vi and Beatrice could have killed them, but the look Rita gave him in return made it clear that he'd be lucky to be let into the house if he kept it up, so he spun on his heels and hurried away.

"What in the world?" Vi asked.

Beatrice leaned back and answered, "He wants the treasure."

"It's so ridiculous." Vi refilled her champagne glass and then laughed again. Gerald had won this round, but he'd opened himself up for revenge, and Vi would bring in both Denny and Victor. Gerald wasn't ready for this, that was certain.

"Smith looked into it a bit," Beatrice admitted. "He wanted to know why the fellow was so insistent. Smith said anyone who was that demanding was half-mad, and he didn't want the man around me while he was gone. Smith made a visit right after I swore I'd tell Rita that the man was looking for her. It'll be interesting to see what happens when Smith realizes Hollands didn't comply."

"Smith." Rita shook her head. She was grinning evilly.

They had moved to drinks and Rita had chosen a simple seltzer water, given her stomach was restless. Vi had gone with more chilled champagne and strawberries and Beatrice selected a G&T.

They relaxed, enjoying the drinks and the music and general atmosphere.

"Our purchases will arrive by noon," Rita said. "We'll have another long hot drive, but we'll be able to go bathing in that pool of yours and see the gents as well."

"We might as well be opium addicts given our need for those boys," Vi muttered. "And the whole reason we left without them was that we were irritated that they were being protective, and here we are rushing home."

"They've missed you too," Beatrice said with the ease of someone whose love only ever pushed her deeper into trouble. The only thing she had to worry about with Smith was whether he would be upset that she didn't do anything devious.

"Oh, stop it." Rita finished her drink as their food arrived. "We'll load the auto in the morning so we can leave as soon as the last of our things arrive," she added innocently as she pulled the plate of oysters in front of her.

CHAPTER 7

*T*he sun was high overhead and the temperature had reached an even more stifling level. It was painfully hot inside the house and everyone had gathered at Vi's by the bathing pool.

Vi swam until she crossed the line from hot to chilled and then begged a cocktail from her twin. He made her one with the same good nature he did most things, and she watched him as he worked.

"What's all this about flitting off to London without Jack?" he asked. "Tired of being married, pretty devil?"

Vi snorted. "Are you jealous, brother of mine?"

"Me?" His eyes shifted. Oh he was jealous, and he didn't know what do with that feeling.

They stared at each other in that way where they silently shared all the things they were feeling. His big dark eyes met hers, and she saw herself in his gaze. In a lot of ways, they were reflections of each other, but their true 'twinhood' was reflected in their innate understanding of the other.

"Are you all right?" she asked carefully, knowing he wasn't.

"I am," he lied.

They both knew he had lied, but she didn't call him on it. They also both knew that he wasn't going to talk about what was bothering him, so instead of pressing she asked low, "What do you need?"

He shook his head and presented her with an icy berry something or other kind of cocktail. She took it with a wide grin and fake laughed, so no one would realize the tension between them. His eyes glinted with gratitude. Her eyes flashed with the promise that once he told her what was wrong, she'd help him solve it.

"Why London?"

"Things for the party and because Jack and Ham had turned on the 'conspiring to protect our girls' switch."

Victor's eyes showed a humor that said he knew better than stifling her under the idea of 'protecting' her. "They're well-meaning."

Vi didn't need to speak to share what she thought of such a statement, which only lent to Victor's humor at her expense.

"I heard Rita telling Ham about some fellow who wasn't leaving Beatrice alone and wanted that prize from the wedding scavenger hunt," he said.

Vi nodded, rubbing her brow. "It's the start of a treasure hunt."

"A treasure hunt." He snorted.

She grinned and leaned in to whisper, "The start is the Goblet of Nemo."

"Like the captain?"

"Like the 'nobody' meaning."

Victor frowned and then laughed. It was like sun breaking through the clouds, and Vi noticed Kate's head jerk up beyond Victor's shoulder. Vi couldn't see her sister-in-law's gaze, but Vi could guess what that movement meant because they were both worried about Victor.

"I suppose the 'nobody' meaning is slightly better."

"It would never fly in a book. Not even the one I'm currently working on, which is terrible."

"When do I get to see it?"

"When I'm ready."

"Since when do we hold back on our books?"

Vi shrugged innocently and noticed the peak of interest in her brother's gaze. It ended too quickly, but it was why she was embarking on this idiotic novel.

"The Goblet of Nemo," Victor mused. "Do you think Rita will let me have it?"

"I think if she does, Hollands might murder you in sheer objection."

Victor frowned and then laughed again. "The great hunter in Africa will come for me in the nighttime?"

"He may well come for you in the daytime." Vi lifted her empty glass to her brother and said, "A treasure hunt should be interesting."

"You don't believe in it."

"That doesn't mean I don't want to see what happens next."

Victor refilled Vi's cocktail and then poured two more. He pressed a kiss against her temple and started away but Vi paused him long enough to say, "Smith broke into Hollands's house and found all sorts of weird things. He told Beatrice he'd be looking further into it later."

Victor's gaze turned slowly to Smith, who was sitting

near the pool while Beatrice, in the water, spoke up to him. There was the slightest softening of Smith's devilish gaze and Vi thought the half-man, half-devil may well actually be in love.

Victor's brows lifted and the same withdrawn look came back over him. The one that said something was wrong.

"You're bored," she whispered. "And you're lost."

Victor gave her a look that demanded silence.

"You're bored and you don't want Kate to know because she's emotional because of the baby. You don't want her to feel as though she's not enough for you especially when she's growing a child within her."

Victor's jaw flexed, and he looked away. When he looked back, his expression told her to stuff it or he'd gag her himself.

His eyes moved from her to his twin daughters and his wife. Kate had decided not to swim, given their next baby had made a bathing costume uncomfortable. She was sitting under a large umbrella with a book on her lap and the posture of a woman who had crossed the line from studious to slumbering.

Vi, however, knew better. She was betting that Kate's eyes were slits, and she was watching her struggling husband with concern. All the brilliance she possessed was focused on the man she loved.

"Keep quiet," Victor hissed, foolishly thinking he'd bypassed letting his wife know that he wasn't well at the moment.

"You're a lucky man," Vi told her brother to see how he'd react.

His response was a kiss on her head again and to try for a

smile. He failed, but he hadn't realized it. He left Vi's side to join Kate under the shade. Vi had little doubt he was avoiding her and her unwanted truths, but if anyone could draw him from his ennui, it was the wife he adored.

He leaned in to examine his potentially sleeping wife. Kate's eyes cracked open and she smiled at him. Vi shook her head. Victor didn't realize, but Vi did.

She turned away, giving them their moments of quiet, and found Jack watching her from the water, so she took her drink and crossed to the poolside lounge chair. Jack pushed himself out of the pool a moment later, and Vi let her eyes rake over her husband as she grinned at him.

His broad shoulders seemed so much wider when she could see them in the light of day. His face had tanned over the last few weeks, and his penetrating eyes had already caught her humor. He was a mountain of man, and he made her feel tiny even when she wasn't particularly small. It was rather like Beatrice and her Smith. When Jack turned all that focus on her? Intoxicating.

"You are a minx," he said, and he didn't even know what she'd been thinking. Jack leaned down to lift her feet onto his lap and sit at the end of her lounge chair.

"I don't know what you're talking about." The lie fell on deaf ears and she could see his mind had already wandered.

When Jack didn't focus back on her, she examined him carefully. His jaw was clenching and unclenching, and his mind was fixed on something that had nothing to do with their lives.

Vi turned her gaze from her husband to his friend Ham and noticed that Ham didn't have that same distant look. He did, however, have a barely pregnant wife who was holding her temples as though she were in pain. Vi's gaze moved back to Jack and she asked, "What's wrong?"

He shook his head.

Her gaze narrowed on him as his eyes met hers, and she could see the flash of humor that ghosted over his face. His eyes glinted, the corner of his mouth twitched, but nothing else showed his amusement.

"You're trying to protect me," she accused.

"It is my job, darling one."

She rolled her eyes at him and leaned back into the chair, lolling as though she were a slug. "It's my job to look after you too."

He pressed his thumb into the bottom of her foot, massaging it. "I won't apologize."

Her look was pure wicked mischief and Jack flinched in the face of it.

He tried, "Come now, darling Vi."

She didn't so much refuse to be placated as refuse to comfort him. She never tried to torment him by getting into trouble or meddling. It was more that she couldn't turn her mind off, and she refused to live inside a gilded cage simply because he loved her. She was as careful as she expected him to be, though. She kept him in her mind when she made her choices but that was what she expected of him as well.

"Jack, I want you to be happy. Follow your instincts and your skill on this case."

He paused and then sighed. "You do have a magic when it comes to getting people to talk to you. You're excellent at figuring things out when you turn your mind to a problem, Vi. But I need to figure this stage out by myself."

She wasn't angry with him, so when he lifted her, laid

down on the lounge chair and tucked her between his legs, she leaned back against his chest despite the heat and told him, "I'm not upset, Jack."

"I just need you to be safe."

She turned to face him, letting her hand slide to where he'd been shot and placed a solitary finger over his scar.

"I know." His eyes met hers with stark honesty. "I—"

"I don't need you to live in a box," she reminded him.

"But you don't want to be in one yourself."

"Exactly."

He tangled their fingers and lifted their joined hands to his mouth. "I love you, Vi."

"And I you," she said low.

A splash interrupted them and Vi laughed as Denny dunked Ham out of nowhere. Ham lazily turned and Denny immediately surrendered, both hands in the air.

"Cowardly lad," Lila called from her own seat in the shade. Her baby, Lily, was laying against her chest and her fan was moving quickly.

Victor dove into the water, joining in Ham's punishment of Denny. They finally left the water when Kate gathered up the babies with the nannies. The group decided to spend the rest of the afternoon napping before a late dinner when the air would cool and they could eat outside on the back patio.

Vi curled onto the bed and Jack tangled their fingers together again.

"I'm not trying to leave you out," he told her again as they snuggled into their bed to nap the hottest part of the afternoon away. "Your safety worries me, and these fellows we've been investigating aren't dangerous, but the next round might be. For now, you'd just be bored. Vi, I won't have other officers. I won't have the weight of the law. It'll be more dangerous, not less."

"All right," she said, having already decided that she needed to let him have his way. "Why are you so introspective about everything?"

"How do you investigate when it's just you?" he asked and she could tell he was bothered. "When you aren't a Scotland Yard officer?"

Vi laughed at him because she knew he was more than up to the task. She curled tighter as she snuggled into her pillow, still eye-to-eye. "Follow your instincts. Look at what Smith does."

Jack's snort had her giggling into her hand and she said, "Maybe you won't get arrested."

"The only reason Smith isn't in Newgate is because he's slithery as a snake." Jack closed his eyes. "I can't get a handle on the man we've been looking into. Nothing makes sense."

"What is he doing?" Vi asked curiously.

"He's disappeared completely. There's no trail to follow. No one knows his history. He's a blank slate."

"Tell me about him," she suggested, but Jack shook his head.

"I'm not ready for that. I need to feel him out in my mind. The fellows who hired us have put a pause on the case anyway. They're not being honest." He lifted the fan to wave it over both of them. "Tell me about this treasure hunter fellow."

"You remember those adventuring brothers from the wedding?"

"Of course," Jack huffed. His disgust was evident when he said, "The men who brought poisons as though it was entirely normal to travel with a Pandora's box full of terror.

Our life is ridiculous. We should come with a warning sign. 'Beware, madness in the vicinity. There's all likelihood that someone has arsenic in their jacket pocket, so don't leave your drink unattended.'"

Vi echoed his sentiment as she added, "They'll be coming to our party. You might want to stay with Ham. That Edward fellow is so…I don't know, Jack. There is something there that is quite odd. I don't like how he's behaving. He crossed the line into almost…fanatical. I'm not sure Ham should be alone with him."

"Well since I don't have a case at the moment," Jack muttered, "I guess I can interfere in yours."

Vi gasped in pretended offense. "Sirrah, are you trying to meddle in my work? What's next? I come to my typewriter and find that you've written several chapters?"

"Don't pretend that you wouldn't love that."

"I won't. Rita is feeling particularly devilish."

Jack lifted a brow and she leaned in and whispered, "She bought a goblet in London. A theater prop to replace the original. She's going to see if he notices."

Jack's chuckle delighted Vi, but there was something else they hadn't talked about yet. She elbowed him without force and then curled into him, choosing to be hotter in his arms than outside of them. "Did you hear Ham and Rita's news?"

"I did," Jack said with the care of a man who was afraid his answer would upset her.

Vi lifted and turned to face him, a frown in her eyes. "And?"

"I don't have an 'and,' Vi. I'm happy for them."

"But now all of our friends will have a child."

"We aren't racing someone to the finish line of life. Our

time will come when it comes, and I'm fine with waiting to have children."

Vi searched his eyes and found that his penetrating gaze was fixed on her equally. She slowly relaxed against him. "As long as you're happy."

He repeated the words to her and it was enough to let her sleep.

CHAPTER 8

"How many people did you invite?" Jack asked as another auto started up the drive.

Vi eyed the incoming clouds from the open window and the darkness that was starting to cover the sky even though they were hours from sunset. "More than five."

"More than five?" His arm snaked around her waist, and he pulled her close to him, laying a kiss on the base of her neck. "Looks like a storm is coming."

"Of course there is," Vi replied. "We're having a party and wanted a midnight swim. I had candelabras placed all around the bathing pool and fires laid."

"Of course," Jack said. "Still, if the heat breaks, I will take it happily."

Another auto approached and Vi grinned as Jack groaned. "Do we even have room for all them?"

"Some will stay at Rita's house."

"And how will they get there after they drink themselves silly?"

"Hargreaves handles things like that, dear Jack."

Vi didn't even feel bad at the exasperation at Jack's face. She turned back to the closet and pulled out her dress. She had gone for a red dress with ancient mythological style embroidery in black. It was made of the softest, thinnest fabric she had been able to find. She added a headband to hold her hair out of her face, not bothering with anything more than mascara, drawing on her brows, and lipstick. Powder and rouge would melt and sweat off in moments and weren't worth the trouble.

Vi grinned at Jack as she turned and then added a spray of perfume with the hopes of smelling like roses instead of rancid sweat.

As she'd dressed, the heat of the day grew weightier and weightier. She joined her friends in the dining room and had a light dinner before the guests started to arrive in force. Hargreaves brought them to the ballroom as he opened the last of the French doors. The heat was astounding, but the chance of any sort of fresh air would help.

As the last guests arrived, so did the first crack of lightning, followed by the snap of thunder. A cheer rose up from the ballroom when a rush of air burst through the room. The breeze smelled of rain and had to be a good twenty degrees cooler.

Vi sighed in relief and jumped up to Jack, wrapping her arms around his neck. "Do you feel that?"

He grinned at her and his schoolboy humor crackled between the two of them. She pressed a kiss on his lips despite their guests.

The band started playing with a long wail of a saxophone followed by a piano and then the low hum of the singers.

Another rush of cool air swirled through the air and their

guests sighed in unison. It was followed by another crack of lightning and a good half-dozen of their guests crossed to watch the storm.

Jack set Vi on her feet and then pulled her into a dance, ignoring those who were flying around the ballroom on roller-skates. With the cool air, their guests spun into the music with the joy of children who'd been let out of school for the holidays.

The relief from the heat was possibly better than the holidays. The heat had been overwhelming for the last few days and Vi had sworn she could see heat waves in the air, but now, she could smell the rain in the air. The scent made her want to head back outdoors and dance in the rain rather than roller-skate in the ballroom. It wasn't just rain, Vi thought, it was chilled rain.

She was pulled from dancing with Jack to Victor. Vi winked at Jack and spun into her brother's arm, asking him, "Well?"

He knew what she was asking. "I'm bored, Vi. Out of my mind. I love my girls, but—"

"They're babies," Vi said. "They're hardly challenging your wit except when you need to figure out why they're fussy." Her agreement gave him permission to feel the way he did.

"Yes." He sounded grateful.

"It's not Kate," Vi said for him, bypassing the guilt that he would feel by even having to say such a thing.

He swung her out and then back towards him. "It's definitely not Kate."

Vi waited.

"It's me. I'm in a mood."

"Perhaps," Vi suggested carefully, "managing the spirits

company and being home most of the time isn't something that you are enjoying."

Victor frowned deeply before he admitted, "Perhaps."

Vi started to reply but her gaze was caught by Jack and Ham stepping from the room with that Hollands oddball.

Victor followed her gaze. "Trouble?"

"I don't think so," Vi replied. The moment she finished speaking lightning cracked again, hitting a tree in the nearby woods. Vi frowned, hoping it wouldn't start a fire. "It's just the treasure hunter," she said, distracted. "They're probably making an agreement to meet him tomorrow and start the treasure hunt. Ugh," she muttered and then tugged him with her to the window. She hoped no one was outside in that lightning. Kate sidled in next to them.

"Oh!" Kate said, nodding out the window as another crack of lightning hit.

A tree in the garden was hit. First there was a slow curl of smoke that was barely visible, and a scent that seemed nothing more than cigarettes across the green of the garden. Then a flicker of flame appeared in the tree. It grew from branch to branch and Vi frowned.

She had loved that tree. "Do you think—"

Before she could finish the thought, Vi saw Jack and Ham pour out of the library doors to the garden. Behind them several servants from the kitchens followed. They were conferring as they walked around the tree, and she stopped worrying what they should do about the fire. She'd happily dump the problem on Jack.

"Shall I go help?" Victor asked and then left before either Kate or Violet could answer.

Vi hadn't realized that the music had come to a stop until

it started again, and a moment later the happy chatter of the party continued.

"He's restless," Kate told Vi. Kate's eyes were suddenly shining with tears, and Vi hooked their arms together. Kate laid her head against Vi's shoulder. "Is he unhappy?"

Vi felt her heart in her throat as she debated answering. If Kate were any other woman, Vi would be fully honest. But Kate was married to Vi's twin, and she wasn't sure what the right course was. Did she tell Kate that she wasn't wrong about Victor being a little off? She paused as she considered what she would want Victor to tell Jack if it were her.

Kate had glanced to the side, and Vi knew she had debated too long.

"I'm sorry," Vi told her, and Kate paled. "No! Not about Victor. I'm sorry I delayed. I got caught in the ethics of being a twin. This is what I can tell you with utter sureness—"

Kate had turned back and recovered color to her face.

"It's something in Victor, not you. He loves you as much as he ever has. It's not the twins. It's not the coming baby. He adores you with all that he is. I suspect that Victor has the same, but lesser, tendency towards grey days that I do."

"But nothing bad has happened." Kate's voice was a plea, and it was painful for Vi to hear. Nothing bad needed to happen to trigger the grey days. They seemed to come when they would, regardless of the time and the location, though bad things did encourage them along.

Vi's mouth twisted and her own eyes were shining with tears. "Having grey days doesn't always have a lot to do with what's happening around us. It's worse, I think, when we know that we should be happy and grateful."

"But why isn't he?" Kate sounded helpless and Vi wondered just how often Jack had felt this way with her.

How often had he looked after her, grey and lethargic, and wished for some way to help her feel better.

"I don't know," Vi said. "Not about why he's having a bad streak or why I have them so much more often. I don't understand it, and the most I can say is that being active—when I can muster it—helps."

"It doesn't make sense to me," Kate sighed.

"I know."

The party moved about them as though they weren't baring their hearts in the corner, and Vi felt the surreal contrast. She waved at a passing waiter who appeared with chilled champagne. She handed one of the glasses to Kate and took one herself.

"What am I supposed to do to help him?"

Vi winced both for Kate and for Jack when it had been Vi instead of Victor. She cleared her throat and then answered as honestly as she could. "I'm not sure."

"Can I be honest with you, Vi?"

Vi nodded.

"Can I ask you to not tell Victor?"

Vi paused for long moments on that one and then she slowly nodded.

"I don't understand what this is about, and it makes me feel helpless."

Vi waited. That wasn't the confession. Not with the sick look on Kate's face.

"And I'm angry. We have so much, and—"

Before Kate could finish the sentence, there was an unholy shriek from inside the house. Vi's mouth dropped open as she looked outside. Jack, Ham, and Victor turned towards the house at the sound, and Vi glanced at Kate. Her hand was on the growing baby, but she told Vi, "Go!"

Vi darted through the crowd, bypassing the roller-skaters to find her way. The scream had come in from outside rather than in the ballroom itself.

"Here, Vi!" Denny called when she reached the hallway, and Vi hurried down the hall towards him.

Denny stood at the doorway to the library and his face was pale, but there was an edge of a smirk to his expression. Until she saw that smirk, she had been sure she'd find a dead body. She followed his gaze to a man in the corner. He was holding a bleeding wound on his head, and he was rocking back and forth.

"They took it!" the man cried.

"They?" Vi asked and then she felt hands on her shoulders. She knew those fingers and didn't need to look up to know it was Jack.

"I was looking at the goblet," Edward Hollands said, pressing at the wound on his head. "Examining it carefully. I was making notes. It didn't, well…"

Vi glanced at Rita as she joined them. She was biting her bottom lip and her eyes were flashing with distinct humor.

Ham pushed past them and handed the man a handkerchief. "Put that against your head, Hollands."

"What happened?" Jack demanded.

A moment later the other Hollands brother arrived. The two of them eyed each other and then the doctor brother took over. "You'll need stitches, Edward. It's not too bad. Head wounds bleed rather fiercely."

"What happened?" Ham snapped. "We left you in here, and now the goblet is gone."

"The thieves must be going after the treasure on their own. They're trying to steal my triumph." Edward sounded half mad.

"I don't think they'll get very far," Rita started.

Denny, however, cut in mischievously. "You have the foremost expert here. Of course they won't."

Given that Edward Hollands wasn't able to look up and see the devilry in Denny's gaze, he didn't realize he was being mocked. Instead, Edward nodded despite his brother's holding his wound.

"What do you think, Shelby?" Jack asked Dr. Shelby Hollands.

"About the wound or the goblet?"

"The goblet," Jack said with the ease of a man who had served in the Great War and knew a medical emergency when he saw it.

"My brother has followed me around the world more than once."

The unspoken tale and the expression in Dr. Hollands's gaze suggested that he didn't have the same faith in the myth of a treasure that matched that of his brother.

CHAPTER 9

*T*he party carried on despite the attack on the treasure hunter and the thunderstorm. Although the story of the stolen goblet spread like mad, no one cared except for Edward Hollands. He carried on and muttered low and then dove so deep into his cups that he was poured into a spare bedroom before the party was even close to done, his brother reluctantly following to watch over him.

For everyone else, things didn't break up until well past dawn and by the time their guests had left, Vi wasn't quite sure why she wanted to have a party in the first place.

Her brother Gerald grinned at her and then went up to his room chuckling. To her butler, Hargreaves, Vi said, "Wake my brother in an hour with coffee and tell him that it's noon."

"What about Lottie?" Jack asked, speaking of Gerald's wife.

"Those are the consequences of marrying a fiend." Vi was

without sympathy for either of them given the headache that they gave her.

"When he figures out the time, send up another servant with a weak premise. I want him to know I was the engineer of his torment and to drive him mad."

Hargreaves grinned and nodded, not even trying to hide his amusement. Jack shook his head and then turned Vi towards him and lifted her over his shoulder, carrying her up the stairs. She yawned against his back and then propped herself up on her elbows to look down to those below. It was only Denny and Hargreaves who watched, which was probably why Jack had relaxed enough to be playful.

"This is the kind of high-handed—" Vi trailed off, laughing against his back. She was a tinge zozzled and it had turned her giggly when combining an evening of excitement with exhaustion. She had danced the night away along with taking a few turns with roller-skates, and she'd enjoyed a bowl full of ice cream, along with lobster and shrimp in various forms. "You know what sounds good?" Her question was finished with a laugh as Jack adjusted his grip on her waist so he didn't lose her.

He bypassed the guest bedrooms that were permanently assigned to their friends and asked, "What?"

"Turkish coffee."

"You need to sleep, love."

Vi laughed against his back. "That won't stop me. But listen, listen."

Jack snorted and then spun her, so she was in his arms like a bride on her wedding day. "I'm listening."

Vi was distracted by his eyes and the line of his jaw and she blinked a few times before she said, "You really do have very firm lines."

He laughed again. "Do you even know what you mean by that?"

Vi shook her head helplessly. "I suppose that a sculptor should like to carve you."

"Me personally or my image in rock?"

It took Vi far longer than usual to follow his thought process and she giggled again. "I don't know."

"You don't know," he said, not bothering to hide his grin. It was wide and amused, and something occurred to her that took too long to haul out.

"Oh!" she said, even though he wasn't aware what had occurred to her. "You're zozzled too."

"Am I?"

"You're grinning like a loon."

His amused expression remained and he didn't dispute her observation.

With a yawn, she said, "Turkish coffee and some of the ice cream. If there is any left."

"Together?" Jack asked.

Vi nodded vigorously and he said, "That does sound interesting."

"That means good," she told him, "but you're always so conservative."

Jack turned and headed back down the stairs, and they poured into the kitchen, surprising the cook, who looked up from directing the post-party clean-up to stare at them. Vi laughed into her hand while Jack tried to explain what they wanted.

"Coffee? Like Mrs. Vi enjoys?"

"Yes," Jack agreed. "With a dollop of ice cream."

"More than a dollop," Vi amended.

"Just enough to add creaminess," the cook guessed.

"An excess," Vi added. "Too much and then a little bit more for good measure."

The cook nodded with the air of a woman who knew who paid her wages and who was also used to her eccentric employers. She gestured to one of the helpers who poured the coffee as Cook dug out the ice cream from the ice box and added it to the cups, putting a dollop on one and almost overflowing the cup on the other.

Vi gasped, blew Cook a kiss, and grinned around a stolen piece of bacon as they returned back up the stairs to their bedroom. She paused half-way to sip on her coffee and then sighed in glee. "I hope this is good when I'm not inebriated."

"It is…enjoyable."

Vi ignored Jack, closing her eyes and savoring her treat before he tugged her after him. They had barely taken another step up the stairs when Vi paused and glanced behind her. "Did you hear that?"

"What?"

Vi swallowed another mouthful of coffee and headed back down the stairs.

"Vi?" Jack called.

"I heard something," she said around a deep yawn. She paused again at the bottom of the stairs and looked over her shoulder at him. "I have the ears of a cheetah."

Jack lifted a brow which made Vi giggle again. She blew him a kiss, took another sip of her creamy coffee concoction, and threw open the door to their library. She gasped when she actually saw someone.

"Hey now!" Vi shouted, her voice even louder from her inebriation and somewhat slurred. "What're you doing?"

The man with a knit cap over his face jerked his head in her direction and then fled out the French doors.

"Vi!" Jack grabbed her arms, pulling her behind him before he darted after the man.

Vi gasped in horror and yelped, "My coffee treat!" as it sloshed out of the cup.

"Hargreaves!" Jack shouted as he rushed through library. "Stay, Vi!"

Vi went to cover her ears at his loudness, spilled the last of her coffee treat, and then found that the cook and one of the footmen had come running.

"Hargreaves went to bed, ma'am," the footman said.

"Jack's chasing a man in a cap," Vi told him, gesturing with the empty cup towards the French doors. She stared down at her coffee-covered dress and pouted, "My treat got spilled."

The fellow stared at her for a moment. "Perhaps you should sit down."

"Cook, will you make me another?" Vi wandered into the library, ignoring her wet dress, and stared out the French doors. There was a noise behind her and she saw the footman had followed. "You look like a mother duck following me around. I'm not a gosling, you realize." She laughed outrageously. "I mean duckling. Or you're a goose. Which one should it be?"

"Ahh," he replied, avoiding her gaze.

Vi snorted and then laughed at the sound of the snort. She looked at the mess of the library, noting that pictures had been removed from the walls and the man had thrown open cabinets and drawers, tossed the pillows from the couches and chairs and turned many over.

"What a mess." Vi frowned and put her hands on her hips. "No one ever thinks that some poor person is going to have to clean up after their thievery."

The footman started putting the pillows back on the couch while Vi collapsed into a chair. "My head is spinning. Please stop moving."

"Ahhh," the footman said again, staring at her and then beyond her as if looking for someone to save him.

"Should I get my brother?" she asked.

The footman brightened at the sheer idea.

"This feels like a Ham situation, but of course, he went home. I wonder if we should call him."

"Perhaps?" the footman replied. He had freckles and they were adorable. His cheeks turned bright red and Vi had to think about whether she might have said her thoughts aloud.

Vi pushed to her feet and crossed to the phone. It took a moment for the operator to pick up and another moment for Vi to remember the number, but she must have asked for the wrong number because the phone rang for ages before someone finally answered, "Hill House."

"Hill House isn't what Ham and Rita named their house, is it?" Vi asked the footman, who had moved to straighten and return books to the shelves.

"No, ma'am," Cook answered from the door, holding a fresh cup, and Vi gasped in joy at the replacement coffee treat.

"Pardon me?" the person on the other end of the line. "Who is this?"

"Vi," she answered with a giggle. "Is Ham there?"

"Ham?" The voice was getting quite angry and Cook suggested, "Perhaps I might take that call for you, ma'am?"

"Ham!" Vi repeated but Cook took the receiver from Vi, and she happily let go to lean back and sip her treat.

Cook murmured into the phone until Vi crowed, "Johnny!"

The footman gasped and turned at Vi's shout and she told him happily, "I remembered your name."

A moment later, Cook rang off and requested another number. This time Vi heard Ham's voice on the other end of the line. "Oh, it's Ham! Do tell him to look for intruders. Someone must have realized Rita was naughty."

"Did you get that, sir?" Cook asked.

Ham's murmur carried over the wire and Vi leaned back with her coffee, waving off the chance to speak to him and curling up with her coffee. By the time she reached the end of her cup, Jack had returned, and she had gone from loud and giggly to repetitively yawning.

"Did you catch him?" she asked through a yawn.

"I did not," he answered, staring at her.

"I forgot Johnny's name."

Jack followed her gaze to the footman and told her, "You're rather drunk."

"I am not. Things are just brighter and louder right now. In fact, my voice is very loud. I don't know why."

"You're drunk," Jack told her flatly and then leaned down to kiss her forehead. "I wasn't able to find the man. What did he want?"

"I imagine the real goblet," Vi said through a yawn. "Rita was naughty."

"Naughty?"

"Well, Edward and Shelby were so demanding. And they kept bothering Beatrice even after they were threatened by Smith. Who ignores Smith's threats? I bet he promised to remove body parts and empty bank accounts. Ruin reputations. Maybe shanghai the men to wherever people get shanghaied to. I bet it was scary." Vi examined her husband

and told him, again, through a yawn, "You're handsome, but I think Smith is scarier."

"Oh really?" Jack asked, taking her cup and pulling her up to lift her into his arms again. "Why is he so much scarier than I am?"

"Because!" Vi laid her head against his shoulder, but then forgot what she was saying. She snuggled into him and closed her eyes. "Tonight was fun."

"Someone tried to rob us."

"But," Vi said softly, yawning hard. "No one died."

CHAPTER 10

*I*t was the headache that woke her. It was followed immediately by a roiling in her stomach that made her regret her life's choices that had led her to that point. Slowly, very, very slowly, Vi turned onto her back and tried holding her head in place.

"It won't work," Jack practically shouted.

Vi gasped and then groaned.

"There's aspirin and water next to you."

Vi reached out blindly and he placed the pills in her hand. She put them in her mouth without opening her eyes and wasn't surprised when Jack pressed the water into her hand next. She lifted her head enough to swallow the pills down and then collapsed, curling onto her side, pulling the blankets over her head.

"Do you want to know what we've found?"

"No," Vi croaked and then groaned again. "Go away."

Jack's laughter followed him from the room.

She closed her eyes more tightly. Her brain, however,

would not turn off. She whimpered lightly and turned from her side to her back, and then groaned as the thoughts assailed her.

First, she'd need to find poor Johnny and give him a bonus and a day off. Then, she'd have to find Cook and beg for another combination of ice cream and coffee because that was a stroke of brilliance that needed to be repeated.

A moment later, however, the thought of ice cream made her gag, and she rolled off the bed and rushed to the bath, making it just in time. When she was finished being sick, Vi started a hot bath and poured herself into it, hoping the scent of ice cream, coffee, and gin would leave and never return.

It took until the water cooled to feel as though she could move without losing her head and even longer before she realized that against all logic, she wanted a full breakfast with bacon, eggs, beans, sausages, and tomatoes. Vi put on the dress she'd been wise enough to lay out the night before. She ignored makeup and put her hair in a turban and left her bedroom with the air of a person who should not be spoken to.

"Vi!" Gerald shouted. He looked exhausted, and despite having a headache from Hades, she grinned wickedly at him. "You're a devil," he accused. "That freckled footman has been knocking on my door all morning."

"Why?" Vi asked innocently, just catching Johnny in the doorway of the library. He must have been straightening it, paused to bother Gerald, and then returned to cleaning the mess the thief made. Vi winked at him and turned back to her brother.

"Don't pretend like you don't know," Gerald grumbled. "Lottie finally told me to leave so she could sleep."

"Heartless," Vi said, but her laugh gave her away.

"This is why Isolde likes me better than you."

"She does not," Vi protested. "She barely knows your face."

"She adores me. And Lottie knows you're a devil now."

"Lottie must have figured that out when she saw me interact with our stepmother." Violet grinned and bypassed him. "You asked for it with Hollands, and you know it. If your lovely wife knows what you did, she'd even agree."

Gerald's expression conveyed nothing and it was enough.

Vi's eyes widened. "You told her!"

His gaze narrowed the slightest bit.

"She told you that you deserved it. Is that why she sent you away so she could sleep?"

Gerald didn't answer, but Vi knew she was right by the way he avoided her gaze.

"You're just like Victor," Vi said, glancing at him sideways and knowing it would irritate him. Gerald loved Victor, but Gerald had the arrogance of an earl-to-be and opinions about Victor's career as a novelist with Vi, his general laziness and lack of decorum, and it was rare for Gerald to realize how much there was to her twin beyond making cocktails.

"You're a brat."

"You started it." Vi had entered the breakfast room by that point and the table was filled with those who had escaped their beds for a solid English breakfast.

Gerald grinned at that and said with pride, "I did."

Vi ignored him to fill her plate.

"I'll end it too."

Vi rolled her eyes at him. "You, brother mine, are a juvenile when it comes to this game. You should consider whether this is a battle you want to begin."

She ignored him once again for the coffee Jack handed her.

"Don't fight with Vi," Jack told Gerald idly. "She'll win."

"You don't think I could win?"

"No. She's meaner than you."

"I'm mean," Gerald snapped. "I could be meaner. Look at these people. They think I'm meaner."

No one met his gaze, but Denny snorted and leaned back with an avid look on his face that said he looked forward to the next act.

"She came up with the not letting you sleep plan while she was drunk and giddy," Jack told Gerald.

"She did not."

"Oh, but she did," Jack muttered. "Why am I arguing with him? Has Ham arrived?"

"Who lives at Hill House?" Vi asked suddenly.

Jack stared at her and Vi shrugged innocently before she said, "I don't think he likes us."

"We were talking," Gerald said, making his own plate and then taking the seat opposite Vi.

"But I got bored," Vi told him. "You're making my headache return."

"You need a cocktail, Vi," Denny suggested, and she shot him a nasty look.

"I'm never drinking again."

"I bet you don't make it one day," Denny said.

"I'll take that bet," Vi countered. "If I win you have to give up chocolate for a month."

Denny gasped, holding his hand over his heart while Jack lifted a significant brow at Gerald. "I told you she was meaner."

"What was stolen?" Gerald demanded, deliberately changing the subject.

"Something was stolen?" Denny asked. "When?"

"You had already dragged off to your bed, Denny," Jack said. "I didn't see anything missing. Other than the goblet earlier in the day."

"They probably returned for the real goblet." Vi sighed into a forkful of beans and told Jack, "I told you Rita was naughty. She bought a prop from some London theater."

"She did?" Hollands asked and Vi looked over.

"Oh, Mr. Hollands."

"It's not gone?" He was breathless.

Vi grinned at him and then glanced around the table, taking note of who was present. Denny was there, along with Smith and Beatrice, her brother and both Hollands brothers. Her cousin Algie waved at her from the corner, with his wife looking nearly as ill as Vi had felt earlier.

"We still have a chance?" Edward Hollands was begging, and his voice shrill and frustrated.

"To find your fake treasure?" Vi asked. "I guess. I don't know what Rita and Ham will do. Let alone Smith. I'm sure he threatened you."

"But he's only…" Edward fell silent when everyone stared at him, some incredulous, some daring him to continue his thought.

"Oh," Denny winced.

"If you want a chance at the treasure, Edward," Shelby Hollands said, "quit infuriating the only people who would let you play."

Edward Hollands turned to Smith and tried a concilia-tory grin, but Smith was unmoved. His cold, snake's gaze was fixed on Hollands, and it was all the more disturbing because of Smith's angelic features and cruel eyes. But when Smith looked at Beatrice, somehow all the darkness disappeared even if nothing else changed about his expression.

"Are Ham and Rita coming?" Vi asked before Edward Hollands started simpering.

"I expect so," Jack replied, refilling her coffee before she did. "Victor as well, I'm sure."

Vi slipped back into quiet, listening to the murmur of those around her as she thought. Her wits were slowly returning. "Who else believes in this treasure?"

"The Treasure of Nemo?" Edward Hollands corrected.

"I can't call it that," Vi replied, pressing on her temples to keep the threatening headache at bay. "The mythical treasure?"

"It's well documented," Edward shot back.

"Using incredibly unlikely sources," Smith replied idly with a low, cool voice that made the others at the table shiver.

Edward was not so wise. "Unlikely? Hardly! I learned this from a professor at Oxford."

"One who no longer works there," Smith added in an insinuating tone that made Edward Hollands's upset seem all the more extreme.

"What do you think?" Vi asked Dr. Hollands.

The man flushed and glanced at his brother. He cleared his throat and said, "Well. The goblet does exist."

"Has it been verified?" Vi asked. "All we know is that Rita's father got it from someone."

"From the family who owned the original property," Edward stated pompously. "There was a strict provision in the family lore that the goblet went with the property. Something that the man who sold the property to Philip Russell felt strongly about."

"But your brother doesn't have the same faith. Does he, Hollands?" Smith accused quietly.

Both of their gazes, along with everyone else's, moved to Dr. Shelby Hollands.

He fiddled with his coffee cup before saying, "We've gone on many adventures, Edward and I."

Smith scoffed and Shelby Hollands added, "Perhaps I am not as convinced as Edward."

"Shelby!" Edward Hollands snapped with a look of pure betrayal.

"It's still fun, though, isn't it?" Dr. Hollands added. "Why wouldn't we chase it? Why wouldn't we try to find it? Do I think that the family buried their treasure and didn't go back for it? Probably not."

"Shelby!"

"Edward, come now. You weren't convinced when you spoke to Gregory St. Claire either."

"Is that the professor you talked to?" Vi asked.

"The St. Claire family owned the house before Philip Russell purchased it," Dr. Hollands explained as his brother crossed his arms over his chest and leaned back with a look that said he wasn't going to be mocked any further. "It was one of the sons of that family who started researching this treasure."

"Why didn't he just chase it down himself?" Smith asked, clearly knowing the answer.

Neither of the Hollands brothers responded, so Smith answered for them. "Because no one in his family believed it. Gregory might be a St. Claire, he wasn't of the main line and couldn't do much at the estate himself."

Denny laughed at that and then rose for a second plate. They all looked a little haggard but Denny's dark circles were a bit alarming.

"What next?" Vi wondered as she leaned back and yawned deeply. "Shall we hunt this treasure?"

"What?"

The door to the breakfast room swung open and Ham and Rita stepped in.

"Oh good," Ham said. "Food."

"We had food," Rita replied.

He ignored her to make a plate while Vi turned and asked, "Well, shall we do it?"

"Do what?" Rita asked, seeing the dirty look that Edward Hollands was sending her way. She knew her trick had been discovered, but she didn't care in the least.

"Find the treasure," Vi answered as she turned to her tomatoes.

"You don't believe in it, Vi," Denny said.

"But that doesn't mean chasing the tale wouldn't be fun."

"Exactly," Dr. Hollands inserted. "The search itself is the joy."

Vi rolled her eyes at the man who had aimed his comment at his brother, who was still looking betrayed. Vi met Rita's gaze as Rita shot Ham a dark look that didn't match how they usually carried themselves. Rita then slid into the chair next to Vi, frowning as darkly at Jack.

"We'll find the treasure," Rita announced.

"Rita, you put that goblet in your dressing room." Ham's tone was furious and his expression said he was questioning Rita's sanity.

"You did?" Vi asked and then laughed. "Good thing. They were looking for it."

"The goblet means nothing," Ham growled. "That fool Hollands was wounded when someone tried to find it. What would they have done to Rita? Or you? Or the baby?"

"The baby?" Denny asked. Rita smiled coyly, but it was no use keeping the secret any longer. Congratulations filled the air.

"Rita and I could find the treasure," Vi stated once they had settled again.

"Vi!" Jack snapped. "We aren't…aren't teams."

"Oh ho," Denny giggled. "Brilliant idea! Can I join the girls' team?"

"There isn't a girls' team," Jack snapped. "That isn't a thing between us. We're all a family."

"Great," Edward Hollands replied with relief, "wonderful."

"Not you," Denny and Smith said in unison.

"It is a thing," Rita replied, but her gaze was fixed on Ham, whose fury had turned his cheeks ruddy. He was so irritated, it radiated from him like the heat over the last fortnight.

"It's a thing," Vi agreed, sipping her coffee happily.

"It's on," Gerald told her as if he were involved. They all stared at the earl-to-be and then Rita's dark laughter turned their gaze back to her.

"It's on," Ham told his wife furiously, and Vi winced for him.

"Oh Ham," Beatrice muttered. When Smith glanced at her, she told him, "We're neutral."

"My bet is on Vi and Rita." Smith wrapped his arm around Beatrice and she scowled at him.

"Jack and Ham are trained investigators." Beatrice was trying and failing to keep the two of them neutral.

"Rita and Vi are criminals at heart. I think we know that

81

criminals win in the end," Smith replied easily, uncaring of frustrating Jack and Ham.

Vi and Rita tapped their cups together, and then Rita rose. "Vi," Rita said, eyeing Ham meanly, "I have an idea of where to start."

"Leave the goblet," Ham snapped.

Rita's reply was cold laughter and the slam of the breakfast room door.

CHAPTER 11

*T*he drive to Philip Russell's home was utterly silent except for the murmuring of Rita. She had taken the auto that her father bought Ham around the wedding, and her fingers moved over the steering wheel as though she were choking her husband.

"You and Ham must have had a rough night?" Vi ventured to ask.

Rita snarled and admitted, "Not really. But then Ham was furious this morning because someone tried to rob us as well. He took it out on me."

"Did he?" Vi asked, betting that he hadn't.

"Well—"

Vi lifted a brow and Rita snarled again.

"Headache?"

Rita's reply was a sniff.

"Did Ham cater to you? Bring you aspirin, let you linger in bed, and worry over the goblet and the house breaker?"

Rita's meek expression was answer enough.

Vi laughed.

"Shut up."

"You know you're going to have to apologize."

"I'm a horrible brat, and I don't want to."

Vi laughed harder, then stopped suddenly. She rubbed her brow and muttered low, "Also, my head still hurts. The aspirin only took the edge off of my headache."

"How did you know that Ham was all…caring and kind this morning?"

Vi's mocking glance was a sufficient reply.

"So Jack looked after you?"

"He often does."

"It doesn't feel smothering?"

"No," Vi said, "but I was rather used to having a kind and loving man look after me before this. I look after him as well."

"It is suffocating."

"Perhaps you're a little—"

"Wrong?" Rita snapped. "I know I am."

Vi's laugh was not the reply that Rita wanted. The drive descended into silence with occasional chuckles from Vi that only escalated Rita's frustration. By the time they arrived at Philip Russell's home, Rita's cheeks were flushed and she had moved to muttering low and viciously, mostly in self-recriminations.

Her father's butler, Baldwin, answered the door and smiled with delight, only to see her expression and then smooth his face into careful evenness.

"I'm sure Mr. Russell will be delighted you've come so quickly."

Rita stepped into the house and then frowned, turning back to the butler. "So quickly?"

"Mr. Russell sent a message to ask you and Mr. Barnes to come. There was a bit of a ruckus last night."

"A break-in?" Vi guessed.

"Indeed," Baldwin said, looking shocked. "How did you know?"

"We both experienced the same," Rita said, moving deeper into the house. She opened the door to her father's office and greeted him.

"Coffee, please," Vi told Baldwin. "She's feeling a bit under the weather and I think coffee might prevent her from murdering us outright."

Baldwin nodded without expression and Vi winked at him, trying for a reaction. Nothing.

"You win this time," Vi told Baldwin. "But I'm making it my goal to get a reaction out of you."

"Of course, ma'am," he told her as though she'd commented on the weather.

Vi followed Rita into Mr. Russell's office and smiled winningly at him. He was in nearly as foul a mood as his daughter. She entered just in time to hear, "—you done? You're playing games with a criminal and here we are again wrapped up in danger."

"You're blaming me?" Rita had moved from inexplicably furious to a volcanic rage.

"You or your friends. Take your pick. I thought Hamilton would be a good influence on you."

"Me?" Rita's voice sounded like it could have come from Medusa. It was a monstrous betrayed fury that could only come from someone whose love had left her to a terrible fate.

Vi took a solitary step back, but it was too late. She'd been seen.

"Lavinia is pregnant, Rita," he reminded her coldly, but Rita ignored him.

"Am I also to blame for your murderous friends in Scotland?" Rita's voice had gone from cold to silky cool.

Her father didn't bother to answer.

"What about Aunt Jean? Is that my fault too?"

It was ludicrous to say so, and the hurt in Rita's voice had him flinching. "I thought I was going to lose Lavinia too. I can't lose another loved one. I won't."

"So you lash out at me?" Rita demanded, her voice cracking. "You bought the house with the ruins and the tale of treasure."

"It was amusing."

"You made a big deal of the goblet. You brought this on us. You did this, and you blame me. Ham blames me. But you know what, it's your fault. And if you lose Lavinia, like you lost Melody, and you lost Mama—that's on you too."

Rita slammed out of her father's office. Phillip Russell slowly turned to face Vi.

"You shouldn't have said that," Vi told him heartlessly.

"I was upset."

Vi nodded, but her expression didn't give him the absolution he wanted. "Rita doesn't need you."

Mr. Russell's mouth dropped open.

"She has me and Ham and Jack and our friends. She learned to get by without you while you were marrying someone her age, while you left her with her murderous aunt, while you focused on your business. I know you were afraid last night for those you love, but you should remember something—"

"Oh really, what's that?" He didn't like being called to account by a woman, especially one he didn't like.

"You're supposed to love her as well."

Vi didn't wait for his reply. Instead she followed Rita to the car and found her crying.

"I need to apologize to Ham."

"Yes," Vi agreed. "You were rather beastly."

"I was horrible. He was afraid for me—for us—you could see it in his eyes."

Vi winced and then told Rita, "Move."

"Move?" she snapped.

"Let me be clear," Vi told her. "We're still on sides against the boys. You and me, my love, we're winning this treasure hunt nonsense, and then we're crowing about it for decades."

Rita wasn't impressed as Vi opened the automobile door and demanded she move to let Vi drive instead.

"First, however," Vi added, "you're apologizing to Ham, telling him you love him, swearing you always will, blaming the baby for your outbursts, and then hopping back into the auto with me to win this thing."

Vi drove back to her house and blared the horn until Jack and Ham stepped out the front door. Jack stared down at her, hands on his hips, as she got out of the auto. There was enough of a smile at the corner of his mouth that she knew he wasn't truly upset.

"Are you being careful?" he asked as Ham approached Rita.

She ran up the stairs to him and wrapped her arms around his waist. "Me? When am I not?"

His snort had her elbowing him and then she said, "I think Rita is a little mad from the baby."

Jack waited and Vi glanced over at two of their favorite people.

"She might also be driving him away so he will get leaving her over with."

Jack pressed a long kiss on Vi's forehead. "I didn't realize how lucky I was that you and Victor knew how to love before I came along."

Vi winked before she said, "That doesn't mean, of course, that I won't be the one who wins this thing."

"Oh-ho," he groaned. "Denny has been whining you left him behind. He went to tell Victor all about your cruelty."

"That's all right. I'll take care of it. Someone tried Philip Russell's house as well," she continued somberly. "They had an intruder. Russell lost all sense of reality and blamed Rita and us."

Jack didn't answer, but by his reaction, he wasn't amused. They both watched as Ham carefully took Rita's face in his hands, said something low, and then Rita nodded against his gentle clasp. A moment later Ham laid a kiss on each eye, each cheek, and then her lips.

"He learned that one from you," Vi told Jack, who laughed.

"Maybe I learned it from him."

Vi shook her head. "Anything that sweet requires love, and Ham has not loved before."

Jack pressed another kiss on her forehead. A moment later Ham and Rita crossed to them.

"Where shall we start?" Ham asked.

Vi gasped in shock. "You would think that these boys would know where to start."

"We know where to start," Jack told her.

"That's good," Vi replied. "Because we're already ahead of you. Come on, Rita. We have a stop to make."

"What?" Ham's mouth dropped and Rita patted him

lightly on the shoulder and then kissed his cheek before stepping away.

"We're still winning, silly," Vi told him and then ran down the stairs to the auto, Rita on her heels.

"That's my automobile," Ham said. "And my partner."

"We're too criminal for you," Vi shot back and made for the car. "We're finding the treasure and wrapping it around ourselves. Like pirate werewolf queens."

"Has she gone mad?" Ham asked Jack.

Vi cuckooed just to throw Ham off, and then hopped back into the auto and rolled down her window so he could hear the sound of her laughter as she sped down the drive.

As they turned onto the road, Rita glanced at Vi. "You made me apologize, which was entirely the right thing to do. Responsible even."

"Don't let it go to your head," Vi said. "Victor isn't feeling well and I think a treasure hunt and general madness will bring him back. And lighten the mood for all of us."

"All right," Rita said easily. "What's a little madness among friends?"

Victor and Kate's house wasn't far from Vi's, though not quite as close as Ham and Rita's. That old mansion hadn't been for sale when Victor had sold his drunken house purchase and bought this one instead. This house was, in fact, much milder.

Vi honked the horn twice, but her brother didn't come out, so she decided to go inside the house and look for herself. Two stories, airy bedrooms, the sound of baby laughter from up the stairs. Her brother was sitting in the parlor, in the dark, staring out the window. Kate stood at the top of the stairs and Vi met her gaze. She had a baby on each hip and a look of sadness on her face. Baby Agnes was crying while Vivi was twisting to get down.

"Victor!" Vi called cheerily. To Kate, Vi said, "I've got a plan." She hurried into the parlor, Rita following.

He looked up, only noticing Vi a moment later. He rose slowly. "Vi." He tried and failed at sounding cheery.

"Victor," she said easily, glancing beyond him to Denny and his worried expression. "I need help. Time to suit up, brother."

"Help with what?"

"Werewolves, pirates, treasure, winning. All of it."

Victor nodded, and Vi didn't need to see it to know he was pretending to be fine. That was fine, she thought. She could work with pretending.

"Do you want to come?" Vi asked Kate as she entered the parlor. Her expression suggested Kate should.

"Let me just leave the babies with Nanny Jane and change my shoes."

"We'll need to switch autos," Rita announced, glancing out at Ham's beloved vehicle.

"I'll get Victor's staid, boring auto." Denny was out the door a moment later.

Victor met Vi's gaze and too much passed between them —essays and monologues, endless communication—all in a glance. It was enough to get him adjusting his jacket and checking his pockets. "Where to?"

"Wherever the madness takes us."

"I'll need to be back for the girls," Kate told Vi. "Maybe I should stay."

Victor shook his head. "Please come." He pulled her close to him and pressed a kiss on her eyebrow.

Vi smiled at Rita. "What is it about the eye kisses? Eyelids, eyebrows."

"Fingertips," Rita added. "They carry more weight for romance than one would ever expect."

Victor looked down at Kate and then lifted her hand to his mouth and laid a kiss on each finger. Kate blushed furiously while Denny groaned at the front door.

"Not in front of other people, Victor. Even I know that. We're ready to go."

"Who knew Denny knew things?" Rita asked.

"A mystery for the ages," Victor said with the first trace of good humor. They all paused too long before Victor groaned. "Let's go already."

"Exercise," Vi told him. "Getting out of the house, counting your blessings, changing your surroundings, and moving until it feels better."

She didn't give him time to reply and rushed down the steps happily shouting, "I call chauffeur! I intend to turn Victor's hair grey and make Denny weep."

CHAPTER 12

"Where to?" Vi asked Rita. "Do you know who you bought the house from?"

"Who my father bought the house from? Yes." Rita reached down to her feet and adjusted a bag that Vi hadn't noticed before. She pulled out a bejeweled goblet and tossed it at Victor. "Decipher clues. The surviving child, Theodette, married Anthony Hill," she said to Vi.

"Hill?" Vi asked too carefully. "From Hill House?"

"Yes," Rita said, "Theodette Hill is…nice, I suppose."

"Nice?" Vi asked. "You suppose?"

"Anthony Hill, he's not, well…"

"New money?" Vi asked, guessing.

"He's from an old line."

"An old line who lost everything by not adapting but hanging onto their arrogance. They aren't going to like us." Especially Vi after her drunken, late night-early morning telephone call.

"But," Rita said, "they're not the only ones we can talk to. There's also an aunt. Harriet."

Vi lifted her head.

"She told me all about the house. Asked to come by and give me the tour and she lives in the village in a pretty little cottage with rose vines climbing the side."

"Did you let her?"

"I told her she could come when we got back from Norway."

"What a perfect day for a tour of your own house."

Rita grinned. "I didn't tell Ham about it. Just said she was a chattering old woman who wanted to talk about the old days, and he didn't ask anything else about it."

"A TREASURE HUNT?" The old woman's eyes were wide and they moved between the group of friends as Rita plunked the goblet down on Harriet's worn table. Slowly, Harriet picked it up.

"This thing." She shook her head and then handed it back to Rita. "Turn it upside down."

Rita turned it over and held it up, so everyone else could see.

"It looks like scratches," Denny said.

"It's been very carefully kept, however," Harriet assured them. "My cousin always thought those scratches were a map, but he could never find where it went."

"Surely it would be in the ruins somewhere," Rita suggested as she poured Harriet Prescott a cup of tea.

"Would it?" Harriet asked with a laugh. Her voice was filled with humor as she looked around the table. "It was my cousin who was the source of all those rumors about it. We looked everywhere." Harriet shook her head and then asked, "Did our stories really cause people to ransack your houses?"

"They did," Vi told him. "I believe your cousin has quite the admirer in a man named Edward Hollands."

Harriet frowned. "You know...I think I've met him. He did love Oscar's stories. Oscar brought him by the house once but of course, Father wouldn't let him see the goblet. Said the goblet ruined Oscar's life, and Father didn't want it to ruin young Mr. Hollands's life as well."

"Did your cousin tell anyone else about the treasure?"

Harriet laughed again and then bit into a biscuit. "Oh that is lovely." In answer to the question, she said, "He told anyone who would listen to him."

"Do you think it's real?" Victor asked with a charm that hadn't been seen for days. "Was this treasure something that existed?"

Harriet Prescott slowly shrugged. She seemed sad when she answered. "There was a time when I believed. There was a time when it all made sense."

"Why did it make sense?" Denny cleared his throat and glanced at the others before he added, "People don't just lose treasure."

Harriet lifted a brow as sassily as any of their friends and Kate choked on a giggle.

"There was a bit of a family ruckus. Imagine the grandfather of the family appalled by the outrageous behavior of his progeny."

"I feel like I know all about times like those," Victor said.

"I think I had one just today," Rita added sourly.

"It's hard, isn't it?" Harriet said. "Choosing what to take from our elders and what to leave behind. What have they given us that we should discard? And what are values that will see their descendants through the ages? In our family," Harriet continued, sounding as though she were no longer seeing them but looking back in time, "my ancestor who supposedly hid the fortune didn't appreciate the idea that he was wrong. He punished the family by taking away the fortune. We were supposedly quite wealthy then. After his death...it was the beginning our decline. The family never recovered."

"Is there any possibility that the fortune of your family didn't just get hidden away by this ancestor of yours?"

Harriet shrugged and leaned back. "Well, that is the question, isn't it? My cousin always believed that this ancestor of ours was too parsimonious, too proud of that fortune and being the lord over it to not leave it intact."

Denny glanced around the table and muttered, "That's what everyone wants but so few have succeeded."

"It mattered when I was a girl, you know. Now—" Harriet shook her head. "My family is gone. So few of us have survived to today, and the family name doesn't mean what it did before. The estate is gone. All of it. We're wisps of memory now, and in another century, no one will care who we were, who we loved, and what we believed."

"Then," Victor told her gallantly, "today is the day you help us find the treasure."

"And," Rita added, "if you'd like, today is the day you return to the house of your kin."

"But it's your house now."

"Perhaps you've noticed that it is ridiculous."

Harriet laughed. "Thank you." Her eyes filled with tears and then she leaned in to admit, "It's drafty and it's yours, my dear. I should very much rather stay in my pretty little cottage. I shall, however, help you find that treasure if only to give my cousin rest."

"Is it possible your cousin is our housebreaker?" Rita asked.

Harriet paused long enough that she answered without answering.

"Is there anyone else that you could imagine also house-breaking?"

Harriet pressed her lips together.

Vi glanced at Rita and asked, "What if we promise not to make things difficult for them as long as we can get them to stop what they're doing? What if you can save them?"

"I'll come," Harriet sighed. "Oscar always was more of a dreamer than someone who bothered with the little things like laws and door locks."

"We can identify with that," Denny told Harriet with pride while the others tried to hide their twitching lips. "We've played with the edges of the law ourselves. Why don't we see if we can find the treasure? Find it and work together?"

Harriet nodded, and Vi took the goblet from Rita, running her fingers over the edges. "It is an interesting set of scratches. It feels deliberate." She looked around the table, and then Vi stood and raised the goblet as she announced, "To Rita's!"

RITA'S HOUSE was sprawling with hallways and wings. It was old and there were ruins of an even older house on the grounds.

"What do we think? Do we think that the ruins are the focus of the treasure or the house?"

Harriet looked up at the house where her mother had been born before walking up the steps. She trailed her fingers over the doorway, seeing something the others could not. With a deep breath, Harriet turned and responded. "It's an interesting conundrum and one we explored both ways. The ruins weren't ruined when the house was built. It was more that they were untenable." She laughed darkly. "So much focus on property, on family lines. My grandfather disowned my mother when she married my father, did you know?"

Rita shook her head.

Harriet continued as if she could see the ghosts of her dead. "Grandfather lived long enough to watch my father die and then my mother die, and he was too cold to do more than see I didn't starve and leave me enough to get by. Nothing more. Economy is always necessary; I have to know my place." She said it like a quote but she didn't sound bitter. In fact, she sounded amused. "The poor man. What a way to live."

"It doesn't make you sad?"

"Sad for what could have been?" Harriet looked up at the house and then away. "I'm too old for that. Though it did make me sad once."

She stared at the property. "Oscar thought that the treasure was in the ruins. He thought that a crumbling mansion and the shadows of the former days would have been the perfect place to hide it."

Victor followed the woman's gaze. "But you have a different thought."

"In those days, I was an audience for Oscar."

"Today you're the star," Victor told her. "We can't do this without you. But, we need to find the treasure, end the hunt, and secure our homes again. We have babies to protect."

"Do you?" Harriet smiled distantly and with real regret. "I always wanted a baby."

"They change everything," Victor told her. He glanced at Kate and took her hand, tucking her into his side. "Family does that."

"Good family," Harriet agreed. "Good friends. I didn't have a child, but I had a good life." She smiled again, this time with pleasure. "I'm old now, and I find myself utterly sure that the twilight of a life should happen with a treasure hunt."

"I couldn't agree more," Kate told her. "Vi, what do you think about the scratches on the bottom of the cup?"

"I think we need a better view."

"Oh," Victor said and Vi winked at him and darted inside, racing up the stairs with her brother at her heels. "Jack will kill me," he called to her, but he did sound worried.

"But not me, so—"

"Devil," Victor cursed and then laughed. True joy was edging into his voice.

They'd passed several shocked servants and other than calling out to ask if Ham and Jack had come back, they didn't stop. Vi found the attic and hurried to one of the dusty windows facing the grounds. She struggled with the warped wood but Victor joined her a moment later and they fought against the old frame together. When the window was open, Vi leaned out, but she couldn't get the view she wanted.

"Don't you do it," Victor warned her, but Vi was already crawling through. He grabbed onto the back of her dress, holding her tightly. "Vi, sister mine, I won't ever get over losing you, but I wouldn't grieve for too long because that man of yours will murder me quickly if you fall."

She kicked off her shoes. "Then don't let me fall." She held out her arm and with a sigh, Victor took hold of her wrist.

"Lean out," she told him.

"Are you mad?"

Vi laughed. "Victor, the view!"

"Vi, your life," he countered, but there was humor in his voice. "Be careful."

Vi took in the scene sprawled before her.

"Do you see anything?" Victor asked, eagerness in his voice.

"I don't know. Do you have a sketch pad?"

Victor laughed and then cursed her. "Don't make me laugh."

"Pull me in," Vi told him. When she crawled through the window Victor lifted her down.

"Never tell Jack," he whispered as if someone were listening.

"That was fun," Vi told him.

He grabbed his heart and said, "Next time I'll climb out."

"But I can't pull you back in."

He made a face. "You aren't the only one who wants to uncover treasure. Always doing the fun parts. Leaving all the work to the gents. Jack is probably chasing the history of the treasure, calling professors, looking at land deeds. Here you are, gossiping and climbing on roofs."

"That's how it goes when you don't have a criminal heart." Vi didn't even sound sorry. "He can live vicariously through us."

CHAPTER 13

"Vi is stealing all the fun," Denny told them when they came back down the stairs. "When we were children, she was the damsel in distress and we were Allan Quatermain. I feel like you've stolen my fate."

"Independent women save themselves," Kate told Denny and Victor before facing Vi. "Did you see anything?"

"I don't know," Vi muttered. "I feel like we could be easily missing lines that have grown over. If the scratches are a map, it could be of secret passageways, the ruins, some path in the woods. We need clues that link the scratches to real life."

"But first," Rita announced, "coffee. My headache has faded, my stomach has improved, and I could use something more than tea and biscuits."

Vi fiddled with her food as they ate; her gaze was fixed out of the French doors, staring towards the gardens. Kate eyed Victor, who said, "We need to get back to our girls."

"I should like to nap," Harriet told the others. "I find that little provides more pleasure than a nap in the afternoon. My grandfather didn't understand the luxury he was giving me when he provided enough to allow me a lifetime of naps."

They finished their lunch in good spirits and Vi took everyone home after wishing Rita a good afternoon. Victor drove them back to his house and told her as she slid into the driver's seat, "Maybe don't tell Jack about the roof?"

"Who, me?" Vi asked. "Do I look ineffably stupid?"

When Vi reached the cottage to leave Harriet, she asked, "Do you need anything?"

"I shouldn't say no to a delivery of fish and chips and a bit of ice cream."

"I do like you," Denny repeated. "You are my favorite type of person."

"Am I?" Harriet asked easily, entirely comfortable in her skin. "Why?"

"Naps and food are the great pleasure of my life as well. Save for my daughter and my wife, of course."

"Of course," Harriet repeated and walked towards her house. Denny walked alongside her and then returned to the auto once she was inside.

"It's just you and me now, Vi. How are we going to use Smith?"

"I hate to break it to you, darling Denny," Vi said easily, "but I think that Smith is more focused on his actual work than our larks."

"Why is he such a spoil sport?"

"Possibly," Vi said idly, "because he does not have a fortune of his own."

"Interesting theory," Denny laughed.

Before long, they reached her house and Vi stopped the auto. They'd have to swap vehicles around at some point, since she was in Victor's and Ham's was with her twin. It was amusing, actually, and Vi wondered what Rita would tell Ham about his missing auto.

The moment she stepped out and turned to close the auto door, she heard rushing footsteps and then a bag was thrust over her head. She gasped and tried to fight, but the person lifted her off the ground as though she were a stray kitten. One hand was placed over her mouth, the bag suffocating her so she was unable to scream, as the arm clenching her too tightly around the ribs hauled her backward.

Vi heard Denny's, "I say now!"

She was dragged—somewhere—fighting as hard as she could and getting in a few good kicks, though not enough to free herself. Finally, she was thrown to the ground with more force than was strictly necessary. Probably in retaliation for those few good kicks. She had enough sense to realize the ground was actually a wooden floor before the arm snaked around her again, and then, a moment later, what might have been the end of a pistol was shoved against Vi's head.

She stilled herself and asked carefully, "What do you want?"

The someone, a man, demanded, "Where is the goblet?"

Vi didn't answer immediately, and she heard the sound of a thump and a groan that she recognized as Denny's from the many times he moaned and groaned in complaint. This time, however, it was in true pain and she heard his knees hit the floor. Vi was instantly afraid for her friend. A bit for herself if Denny's presence meant no one knew they'd been taken.

"Don't be stubborn, woman," the man snapped. "Where is the goblet?"

"Don't tell him anything, Vi," Denny shouted and then grunted again. With a weak gasp, he breathed, "Bloody hell."

Vi didn't answer. Instead, she demanded, "What are you thinking?"

"Did you search the car?" the man holding her demanded.

Vi heard a groan from Denny and she tried not to think about what it meant.

"Of course I did," a second voice answered.

"Nothing?"

"I would have told you," the second voice groaned.

A third person said, "They're going to see the auto and come looking." This voice was younger and had a slight rasp, and he sounded far more worried than the others.

"She's notoriously unpredictable," the first voice said. "It will take time for them to be truly worried."

Denny laughed even though she could tell he was in pain. "That's what you get for your devilry, Vi."

Denny groaned again and Vi tried to jerk away from the fellow holding her but failed. His fingers dug in hard, and she had little doubt they'd leave bruises.

"You don't want to hurt us," Vi tried. "You don't want my husband to filet you."

"I already have," the man said. There was the sound of another thud and Denny groaned.

"By Jove, man," Denny yelped. "Would you stop? We don't have your cup. Obviously."

"Oscar?" Vi asked and a sudden silence told her what she needed to know. She couldn't see them and they couldn't see her expression, so they didn't know they'd given themselves away.

"Where is the goblet?" he demanded again. "We know you had it today."

"We don't have the cup now," Vi snapped. "So, what's your plan?"

It was obvious where it was if Vi and Denny didn't have it and reasoning must have caught up with the three who were holding them. Vi heard another thump and another groan. This time the sound of a body hit the floor.

"Do I have to hit you as well," the man holding her threatened, "or will you remain here like a good girl?"

Vi didn't bother to answer the fiend, but she intended to show him exactly what kind of 'good girl' she was. Before she could move, however, someone grabbed her wrists and bound them and a moment later, a wooden door slammed shut.

Vi yanked at her wrists and she had enough give to snake them under the hood over her head and shake it off. She bit at the loosened bonds and got them off her wrists and then rushed to Denny. He was on the ground and unmoving.

"Denny," Vi groaned. She knelt next to him, checking his pulse. She felt the beating of his heart and turned him onto his back.

He groaned and Vi gasped. "Denny? Please be all right."

He didn't awaken, but he was breathing and not bleeding. She pressed her hands against his face in apology and then pushed up to her feet. Denny needed help.

SHE TURNED and took in her surroundings. They were, she thought, in one of those outhouses near the side of the garden. Vi tried the door, but it wouldn't budge. The vague memory of noises after they'd tied her must have been the men locking her and Denny into the shed.

She muttered an insult and turned, taking in the small window.

"It seems, dear Violet," she told herself, "you haven't finished climbing out windows today."

The light was low, but there was enough to see that they were in a gardening shed. It took a moment to find a heavy shovel. She slammed it through the window, knocking out as much of the panes of glass as she could.

"Hello!" she shouted. Her voice was rougher than she thought it should be.

No one replied, so Vi grabbed the hood that had been placed over her head to protect her hands as she crawled through the window. When she was half-free, Vi saw someone heading towards her end of the garden. Someone had heard her. She laughed in relief when she recognized the footman and tried to call, "Johnny."

Her voice was weakening from the pressure of the window frame on her abdomen, however, so she slithered out of the window and landed hard in the dirt before she could shout again, "Johnny!"

"Mrs. Wakefield?" She heard the shock in his voice and rolled onto her back. Her dress had ripped, and her forearms were bloody as she pushed up onto her hands and knees. Johnny reached her and pulled her up.

"What happened?" Johnny gasped.

Vi shook her head and lurched towards the shed door. "Help me with this door. Denny is inside."

"Ma'am?"

"Denny!" Vi shouted as though Johnny would understand if she was louder. Then she saw Jack coming out of the house. "Denny! Jack, help! It's Denny!"

Jack knew the tone of Vi's voice when she was in true

distress, and he rushed towards her. As he ran across the green, she shouted, "Denny's in the shed, Jack. We were ambushed."

"Is he alive?"

Vi nodded and tried to answer at the same. Jack reached her and then moved past her, kicking at the jammed door.

"Call a doctor," he ordered.

Vi gasped and hurried past Jack, running for the house with the gait of an injured antelope. She staggered up the steps and through the door when Johnny caught her when she would have fallen.

Of course Jack meant for Johnny to run to the house, not her, but it was too late now.

"Mrs. Vi!" Hargreaves gasped. Vi took his arm, leaning on him. She must have injured her ankle.

"The telephone," she said.

Hargreaves nodded and helped her to the library. Johnny was already there and had the operator on the line. Vi telephoned Rita first and warned her of the danger. The second she ended the call, Vi gave Hargreaves the telephone and asked him to call the doctor and then bring Lila down.

Vi limped to the front of the house, conscious of the fact that Johnny was trailing behind her once more like a mother duck, and found Jack carrying a half-aware Denny inside.

"What happened?" Jack demanded as he laid Denny on the Chesterfield in the parlor.

"Those mad men seeking for the goblet thought we had it. They grabbed us the moment we left the auto and were rather rough with us."

There was a fury in Jack's gaze that Vi hadn't seen in quite some time. "Are you all right?"

"They put a hood over my head and told me to be a good

girl. So, I'm furious. Beyond that, I'm just a little scratched up and bruised." She tucked her arms close so he wouldn't see the blood right away. She needed him clear-headed and not charging off in a blood-boiling fury.

Vi watched his jaw flex over and over and then he glanced past her as Lila arrived.

"He'll be fine, Lila."

She hurried across the parlor and knelt next to Denny. Her big eyes were wide with concern as she looked back at Vi and demanded, "What happened?"

"We got back from our day of hunting treasure, and they must have thought that we had that goblet. Jack—"

He shook his head at the plea for… she didn't even know what she was looking for. She just wanted to feel as though the last half hour hadn't happened. Vi shivered and rubbed her arms, forgetting the scratches and blood, but the sting was easy to ignore.

Vi's gaze turned to Lila. "I…Lila…I…they asked me the questions. When I didn't answer, they hit him. I'm sorry. I didn't want to send them to Rita."

"I understand," Lila murmured. "We'd have done the same for you and she for us."

"I'm sorry, Lila. I should have—"

"You should have what?" Lila sniffed and gently took Denny's hand. "You did the right thing. The good news is that Denny has a hard head. He'll be fine, and you'll find the ones who hurt him for a goblet and fictional treasure. It's… it's…stupid. We will make them pay."

The last was said to Jack, and he agreed.

"What happened earlier in the day, Vi?" he asked a little too calmly. He must have seen the scratches.

"Nothing that felt useful. We had fun, but—"

"There must have been something."

Vi pressed her fingers to her aching temples. "Rita knew someone from the family. We visited her and invited her to the house. She told us about the family, and we looked about a bit. There are scratches on the bottom of the goblet," she added.

"That doesn't sound all that useful," Jack muttered. "This whole thing is just…just…"

"They believe it," Lila said from her position on her knees, her hand slowly pushing back Denny's hair. "They believe in the treasure."

Jack grunted. "You're right. It's real to them. And people murder over far less than a mythical treasure." Jack carefully reached out and took Vi's hands in his. He turned her wrists over and looked at the scratches.

Vi bit on her bottom lip. "We talked to Harriet Prescott. She didn't believe in the treasure. Not really. Her cousin Oscar is the believer. He's always believed. He was the one who told Edward about it."

Jack nodded. "This just got significantly more dangerous." He let go of her hands, curling his into fists and breathed deeply. Striving, she thought, for patience.

"I know," Vi said simply. "I called Rita and Ham and warned them. Ham wasn't home yet."

"I don't like how we're separated," Jack affirmed. "We're more vulnerable this way."

Their gazes met and she could see all of the worry and the fear and the burning rage in his gaze, and he could see, she hoped, her love and her trust in him.

"We have to find the treasure," Vi told Jack. "Or discredit the possibility of it. That's the only way to end this."

His jaw was flexing again, and his fury was barely

contained. Vi didn't reach out, knowing he needed to gain control before he'd find comfort in her touch.

"We have to find both the treasure and the man who did this," Jack told her. "Otherwise that house isn't safe for anyone."

Vi stepped back and gave him space. He eyed her, and she could see his anger increase with her retreat. He turned and slammed his fist into the wall. It wasn't clear if the sound woke Denny or if he'd awoken and had been watching, but Jack's fist through the plaster had Denny hooting a weak laugh.

Lila's laugh echoed Denny's and there were tears in her voice when she said, "He'll be fine." After a long pause, she added, "Until I kill him."

Vi's head tilted at her husband who had pressed his face to the wall and was breathing slowly. "Do you feel better?"

He sighed into the wall and countered, "Are you truly all right? You aren't going to have nightmares?"

"I like your hands," she told him easily, "so I suspect I might. What will I do if you turn your fingers to mush by pounding the wall and I have to feed you? If that happens, I can promise you, dear Jack, that I will ensure your food is always cold."

His arm snaked out and slid around her waist, pulling her close even though he still pressed his face against the wall. His gentle handling of her was completely opposite of the fiend that had pinned her down. "We discovered nothing. You learned nothing?"

Vi cupped his jaw and whispered into his neck, "Please be gentler with yourself."

"What did you learn?" he asked again. "There must have been something."

"Only that the story of the treasure is shaky. The idea that there is significance in the scratches someone carved onto the bottom of that goblet? Maybe." She leaned into him, pressing her cheek against his chest and listening to his heartbeat. "It looks deliberate if you stare at it long enough. But Harriet Prescott and her cousin looked for the treasure for years and found nothing."

"It's ludicrous to imagine that the treasure exists," Jack snapped. He wasn't angry at her, and she wasn't offended. That snap in his voice matched her own feelings.

"We find it," Vi told Jack and then her head tilted as another idea struck her. "Or we fake finding it."

CHAPTER 14

*V*i sat on the stairs outside of the parlor while the doctor checked Denny over. While she waited, Hargreaves hovered over her and Jack spent some time on the telephone in the library. By the time the doctor left Denny for her, Jack was done and joined Hargreaves in his hovering.

"Where are the Hollands brothers?" Jack asked Hargreaves while Vi pretended that she didn't want to jerk her hands away from the doctor.

He cleaned and examined her scratches while Jack saw every wince with those observant eyes of his.

"They left this morning after you didn't allow them to go with you."

Jack breathed in deeply and then told Hargreaves, "Call the inn. They can have a room for two nights that we'll pay for, but beyond that, they're on their own."

Hargreaves nodded and then paused. "I heard your phone

call, sir. Johnny and Cook can keep an eye on the house. I'd like to come and help."

"Of course," Vi answered for Jack and then gasped from a stinging pain. She hadn't been prepared for that and both Hargreaves and Jack turned instantly. "I'm fine!"

"She's fine," the doctor agreed. "Just a little burn from cleaning the wound. She doesn't need stitches, and I'll bandage it, but it's a precautionary measure."

"Don't tell them that," Vi hissed in a deliberately loud whisper. "They'll spoil me if you don't ruin it."

The doctor laughed and patted her on the head. "I suspect they'll spoil you regardless."

Vi smiled at the doctor and then glanced around. They'd gathered an audience. Most of the lingering guests from the party had left, but Gerald and Lottie were still there along with Smith and Beatrice.

Jack followed her gaze around the room and said, "This treasure hunt has become dangerous. You need to choose between going with us to Ham and Rita's house or going back to London."

Beatrice placed her hand on Smith's arm, but her eyes were fixed on Vi. "Are you all right?"

"I'll be fine," Vi said, but she shivered deeply and knew that Jack had seen it. She tried to hide the building reaction, but she wasn't quite able to. Vi couldn't shake the feeling of that gun on her head, and even though her friends were talking quietly, she was hearing the sound of the fists striking Denny again and again.

Vi closed her eyes and breathed in, trying to focus on the sounds of the voices around her. Where is the goblet? Then the thud. Denny's groan. Vi wanted to put her hands over her ears and block it out, but she couldn't because it was echoing inside of her head rather than in the room.

The doctor said something to Jack, but Vi was only hearing that thud and the sound of her breathing in the hood. Where is the goblet? Vi reached out blindly and took Jack's hand and with his warm grip, she felt like herself again.

Whatever had been decided while Vi was locked inside her own head had ended, and to her surprise everyone but Jack had gone. He knelt in front of her and took her face in his hands. "Violet?"

She started to tell him she was fine, but instead, she leaned into his arms and wrapped herself around him, needing him to hold her to remind herself that she wasn't in the shed with a gun against the top of her head. She hadn't told Jack about the gun. She couldn't.

Vi breathed slowly out and to her surprise, it was a weak hoot. The sound you made before you dissolved into tears.

"I'm all right," she lied.

"Of course you are," Jack lied in return and then he lifted her once again, carrying her up the stairs. She expected him to curl himself around her when he set her on the bed, but instead, he packed their things. He was careful to get her current manuscript and her cosmetics, her favorite jewelry she fiddled with when she was worried. He carefully closed the drawers and cabinets, leaving their bedroom perfectly in order, so the mess didn't disrupt her peace. The whole time she had her arms wrapped around herself and she watched numbly.

"Take a quick bath and change, Vi. If Victor sees you covered in dirt and blood with a ripped dress, he'll lock you in the cellar until this is over."

"We're going to Ham's?" Vi rubbed her brow, knowing the answer already. It was like her mind was on delay, and she wasn't quite sure why. She was fine. She hadn't been hurt too badly and yet it felt as if she had been.

"When there is trouble, we gather together," he reminded her. "These fellows were only able to do what they did because we had separated."

Vi nodded and then rose. She cleaned herself quickly, mindful of the bandages, and dressed without paying attention to what she wore. Finally, she took her sweater from the back of her closet. She was shivering and she needed to help. Only, Jack had done everything needed and what she ended up doing to move things along was pick up her journal and her dogs. Vi put one dog under each arm and followed Jack down the stairs.

"Is she all right?" Gerald asked Jack as her elder brother loaded his own auto. Vi was surprised to see her brother carrying his own luggage.

"I didn't know you ever did manual labor," Vi told him.

"She's just a little upset," Jack answered for Vi. "Anyone would be."

"It must have been hard to hear your friend being hurt." Lottie ignored Gerald opening the auto door for her and went to Vi, hugging her carefully. "It'll be all right, Vi."

Vi nodded, thankful for Lottie's warm embrace, then pulled away as Hargreaves drove another auto up to the house. She heard a noise and glanced at the house to see Denny pretending each step didn't hurt as he made his way down to the drive. Lila was a step behind her husband with baby Lily in her arms. Lily's big blue eyes were fixed on her father as though she knew that he was in pain, and her gaze was as worried as Vi's.

Vi reached for Lily so Lila could open the back of the auto for Denny. It felt good to have a baby in her arms.

Denny got gingerly inside and then looked up at Vi and Lily. "Are you all right?"

"I'm fine," Vi told Denny. "You?"

"Fine," he replied and then laughed. "We're both liars. Did you tell him?"

Vi shot Denny a dirty look.

"Tell me what?" Jack asked as he joined them.

Denny laughed low. "I thought not. He doesn't look nearly murderous enough."

"Vi?"

She looked at Jack and then at Denny and then said, "Don't worry about it."

"Did they hurt you?"

"You saw the extent of my injuries."

"They put a gun to her head, Jack," Denny told him. "She's out of her skin because she realized murder—for her—was a breath away."

"Why didn't you tell me?" Jack asked, and the pain in his voice was enough to make hurting him a thousand times worse.

"Because," Vi answered softly, "I realized that I could lose you when the gun was to my head. I realized again, later, that I could lose you if you were taken to Newgate for murder."

Jack's gaze fixed on hers, and he saw the truth in it.

"I would rather carry this alone than lose you, Jack. You being protective makes me feel safe. I love you for it. I will protect you back. And Denny." Her gaze moved to him and she put the baby in his arms. "I'll hit you twice when it doesn't hurt so bad."

"It's not just Jack you have to worry about," Denny told her, uncaring.

"Victor will control himself."

"He means all of us, idiot," Gerald told Vi, and she stared in shock. "Don't look at me like that. I've lost two siblings so far, Vi. I'd prefer to keep the rest of you."

"Go home, Gerald," Vi said. "Don't you know we're cursed? Save Lottie from us."

"We aren't leaving," Lottie exclaimed.

"Yes, we are," Gerald replied. "Jack will take care of Vi and the rest. Thank the heavens, our troublesome Vi and Victor have gathered Jack and Ham about them. Inexplicably."

"Inexplicably?" Vi demanded.

"Well, Denny makes sense, doesn't he?" Gerald asked. "He was the perfect tagalong for you and Victor as children. Jack, though, he must have been pretty bored when you met him."

"Bored?" Jack asked.

"Why else would you join Vi and Victor in their madness? Traipsing around the world, interfering in your cases, roller-skates parties. It's shocking to me they haven't burned a house down yet."

"There's still time," Vi said, but she felt better. What was it about being scolded by someone that she loved that made her feel loved in return? She might be a little broken in her mind. "I'm not sure Ham and Rita love their house like they should."

"Harriet did say it was drafty," Denny said. "Maybe we should create another round of ruins and help them design a new house."

"With secret passageways," Vi added.

"And maps scratched onto the bottoms of goblets."

"Are you staying?" Jack asked Gerald. "We need to get to Ham and Rita."

"Yes," Lottie said.

"No," Gerald countered. "It isn't just Rita who is expecting, and we won't risk my heir for buried treasure."

"Gerald," Lottie said.

"He's right, Lottie," Vi said. "Also, I have an idea."

"An idea?" Gerald shook his head and placed his hand over her mouth. He leaned in and kissed Vi on the forehead before he added, "We're leaving now, Lottie. Jack and Ham are soldiers. I, however, am not."

Vi kissed her brother on the cheek and then took a seat inside the auto. A moment later, Jack got behind the driver's wheel, and they made their way to Ham's house, leaving Gerald and Lottie to make their way back to London.

Vi thought that Jack would be furious, but instead, he held her hand during the drive, rubbing his thumb carefully over her palm.

She was relieved to see Victor standing on the steps on Ham's house. He was worried. Vi didn't need to meet his gaze to know. It was there in the line of his body, the way his shoulders were slanted as though he were both waiting for her and blocking the door against intruders.

"Vi?"

"The house is secured?" Jack asked, taking Lily himself and handing the baby to Vi so he and Hargreaves could help Denny from the auto and up the steps.

"Do we really need to act like this?" Victor asked, but Vi could see that he wouldn't take the risk. "Smith and Beatrice arrived and Smith went for the guns and the doors. He locked us in like we were going to expect a company of artillery."

"He had Beatrice with him," Vi told Victor.

"They put a gun to Vi's head," Jack finished.

Victor shifted again and she shook her head as she saw the look on his face as she stepped into the house. She found Kate and Rita inside the doors with Beatrice just beyond them.

"What's this about a gun to your head?" Smith asked. He saw the baby in Vi's arms and said, "We moved the nursery to a little-used guest room at the back of the house, just in case."

"This does feel like an overreaction."

"It probably is," Ham said, his gaze moving from Vi to Jack and then back to his wife. "What we're actually dealing with is an over-eager madman who believes in this treasure."

"And believes he was robbed," Smith added. "I did a fair amount of investigation in the last day. Bea and I did," he amended with that look he got when he spoke of Beatrice.

"And?" Jack demanded.

"The old man who owned this house mocked the unfortunate grandchildren with it. He was a right bastard. The worst sort of mean. For them, it's not about the money or the gold, it's about winning against a man who tormented them the whole of their lives."

"Who are we dealing with?" Jack asked.

"The three grandchildren were Harriet, Oscar, and John Prescott. John is dead, but—"

"John had two sons?" Vi guessed, thinking of the second and third voices. The one who had searched the auto and the one who had been worried that others would come. To her surprise, she felt sorry for all of them.

CHAPTER 15

"It's moments like these," Victor said, "where I find myself grateful for Father just being entirely absent. Poor chaps. Must've been hard."

"My father would have made the old man with his cruel treasure hunt seem like the fairy godmother," Smith told Victor, shaking his head. "There's no excuse for breaking into a man's home."

Vi bit her bottom lip, but she couldn't stop the laughter from escaping. Everyone turned to her and then glanced at Smith who, to her shock, winked.

"Ironic?" he demanded.

"Possibly," Vi agreed and then took in the gathered force. "I shall endlessly be grateful that you all are my family. And speaking of family and the strength we give each other, where's the goblet?"

Rita crossed to the grandfather clock by the door and opened its cabinet, pulling out the cup. She tossed it casually to Vi and Vi looked at Jack. "I have an idea."

To be honest with herself, she expected him to put her in the nursery with the babies. The worry and love in his gaze was pained when he nodded and she grinned at him.

"To the roof."

"With a rope," Victor called as Vi and Jack started up the stairs.

When they reached the attic, Vi showed Jack the window, and he shook his head. "It's too narrow for me, Vi."

"We need to go higher," Vi pointed to the roof. "This goblet is a few generations old, right?"

Jack nodded. "Ham and I verified that. There are credible stories from around the village. People who saw it as children or heard of it. The vicar laughed far too long about the name, but he agreed that it had been around for a while."

"So, the map, if it is a map, must be of something that would last," Vi told him. She handed Jack the goblet and then leaned out. He, like Victor, grabbed the back of her dress. "Look, Jack, do you see it?"

He wasn't looking at where she was pointing, he was looking at her face. "You seem better."

"I'm fine," she told him and this time it wasn't a lie.

She turned in his hands and faced him instead of the land below. She took his face between her hands as he had done so many times, rose up on her toes, and she placed a kiss on each eyebrow, then each eyelid. When she went for the tip of his nose, he laughed, and she was beguiled by the edge of his mouth where all his humor lived.

"Jack—" There was longing in her voice, and his fingers dug deeply into her spine.

"Vi," he countered, and she got the kiss on the tip of her nose instead. "We're going to the Amalfi Coast after this. Just the two of us."

Vi shook her head and confessed, "I told Gerald—"

"Then we'll go back to one of those Spanish islands or to Cyprus or to a Hawaiian Island, and we'll linger in the sun and avoid killers and people who would dare—" He took her face between his hands as well, and they were tangled together when Ham entered the attic.

He took in the sight of their tangled forms and said mildly, "There are bigger windows on that side of the house."

Vi let go of Jack's face, but he leaned in and placed another kiss on her forehead before they followed Ham to a larger window, which opened as though it had been recently oiled. So, Victor had confessed to Ham what they had done. Vi didn't know how to feel about that, though she was grateful that Ham was prepared.

Ham held a rope in his hands and Jack took it, tying it around Vi's waist, and then watched as she kicked off her shoes and peeled her stockings away. A second rope was placed around Jack's waist and Ham anchored them to a support post in the attic. Vi loved them both in that moment. She knew neither wanted her to go out that window, but instead of arguing, they silently helped.

Before Vi was able to climb through, the others joined, except the nannies and the babies, and Victor shook his head at Vi's mischievous grin.

Vi went first, since she was smaller and could test the strength of the roof. Jack followed after and she crawled towards the peak of the house with the goblet secured inside of her dress, sure of his strength to keep her from falling. She moved up the roof easily and then took a seat by the top part of the house. They could see for miles and miles and much of the land was covered in trees that had stood for as long as the house.

"How lovely," Vi said, looking at their house in the distance. It hadn't been there as long as Ham and Rita's home, but it was a noble old thing all the same and all the more beautiful for being the place where Jack had been raised and where they would someday raise their own children.

Vi fished the goblet out of her dress and then realized that Jack had stiffened next to her.

"Smith! Ham!"

"Jack?" Smith answered with casual ease, poking his head out from the window.

"In the trees at three o'clock. Can you see them?"

"There's an auto there," Vi gasped, turning away from her own house. "There shouldn't be an auto there."

"That's part of the land between Ham's house and ours," Jack agreed. "It seems they've made themselves at home."

"How long, I wonder, have they been living in our woods?"

"Has anyone checked the ruins?" Victor called. "Perhaps Ham and I should do that."

"We stay together," Jack countered. "At least, we stay together and move slowly towards our objectives."

"Agreed," Ham added. "They're fools, but they're armed fools. They're far more dangerous than criminals at this point."

"Look," Vi said, turning her attention, but not her hand, to what she was trying to show them. "Look at the river and look at the goblet. The first house wasn't so far from that curve in the river, and there is a slightly bigger gouge there. It looks almost accidental."

"But not," Jack agreed with that winding curve.

"They must have thought of this before," Vi told him

softly. "They've been looking the whole of their lives. They're missing a key piece of information and I seriously doubt we've uncovered it. We have to assume we're behind them."

VI CLIMBED BACK through the window and Victor helped her in, Jack following after her. Victor took the rope from around her waist and crawled out to see what there was to see while Vi faced the others.

"They didn't shoot me when they could have, and they didn't do more than bruise Denny."

"I don't care," Ham told her flatly. "This is my home. That is my wife. My baby is on the way and if they were to have done that to Rita, our child might not have survived. I'm not saying I'll shoot them in the head like they threatened to do to you, Vi, but I'm not feel very generous."

Vi nodded and then said, "I vote for checking the ruins."

"I as well," Rita agreed.

She shifted and Vi gasped. "Is that an elephant gun?"

"It's what I used in Africa," Rita agreed. "Lions are a serious business, you know."

"You're never going to Africa again," Ham said. "I didn't even have such a thing on the battlefield."

"I'm never going alone," Rita agreed. "There is this place with giraffes. Ham, you'll be forever changed."

"Giraffes?" His disbelief was clear.

Rita patted his cheek lightly and repeated, quite seriously, "Giraffes."

"We'll all go," Vi announced grandly and everyone groaned.

"Our luck is too bad," Victor told her. "We'd certainly be trampled by giraffes right after they changed us forever."

"Don't you want to see the sun rise over the savannah? Don't you want to see where Tarzan swang?" Vi demanded. "How many books do we have to read before you realize my needs?"

"Tarzan isn't real, and don't you want to go to Mars as well?"

"Obviously," Vi shot back. "John Carter of Mars is almost as compelling as Tarzan, but alas, Mars is a bit more difficult to reach than Africa."

Victor sighed and looked around for support, but no one else had even been listening to their byplay. It seemed that Rita with her elephant gun was far more compelling than the fictional settings of the Edgar Rice Burroughs novels.

"Have I told you the premise of our new book?" Vi asked Victor when she noticed an edge of the blues in his expression, hidden behind all of that worry.

He lifted his brows in question and waited for her explanation.

"Pirates."

"I feel like we've done pirates."

"And werewolves."

Victor just blinked and then said, "Rita, the elephant gun, and Vi and I are going to the ruins to see if there has been a disturbance."

Jack frowned. "And separate again?"

"While," Victor continued as though Jack hadn't spoken, "you and Ham unite and head towards the auto. We'll leave Denny, Hargreaves, and Smith armed."

"I'm coming with you," Smith said. "Beatrice, however, will be more than sufficient for anyone who dares to break into the house. Don't be confused by her professionalism and brilliance. She's spent enough time with me to also be vicious when necessary."

"Look at it this way, Jack," Victor told him. "We are separating with the knowledge that we might be attacked."

"That doesn't help."

Vi grinned as she led the way from the attic. She changed her shoes to boots, deemed her day dresses suitable, and found that Jack was pressing a pistol into her hand along with a kiss on her forehead.

"Be careful," he said.

"You be careful," Vi told him. Adding quite seriously a moment later, "Also, don't kill anyone and separate us forever."

"We'll just flee the country," Jack told her easily and she considered for a moment and then agreed.

Before they left the house, they gave Kate the goblet and had her sketch out all the details on it she could see. She made two copies and then handed Jack and Ham the goblet. They left the house through the French doors at the back of the house that poured onto a lovely patio with a curved line that stepped down into the garden.

"Now that I look around and think about the fact that Rita is carrying a gun that could end a rampaging elephant, I feel ridiculous," Vi confessed.

Victor glanced at Vi and then told her, "You had someone hold a gun to your head, Vi."

Vi didn't reply right away. Instead she considered. The memory of it was wispier now. It seemed that it had faded in the light of being with family and friends and among those who loved her. It wasn't as though she hadn't been scared before. It wasn't, even, that she hadn't feared for her life before or that it hadn't affected her. But, when it came down to it, this time it wasn't lingering.

"I don't think they were going to hurt me."

"Because you're all right now?" Victor cursed and Vi lifted a brow with a glance at Rita.

"Because it was alarming in the process, but I don't have this lingering fear like I do from other circumstances, Victor. I would be terrified if I saw Preston Bates today because I know he would hurt me if he could. He followed me and terrorized me. This Oscar fellow didn't make me terrified in that way. It wasn't personal."

"But it might be, Vi," Smith warned, "if you had his treasure. Don't trust your instincts too far."

Vi glanced at Smith and realized he was right, and she was wrong. She fiddled with her wedding ring and remembered that this Oscar fellow could have easily taken her forever from those she loved. Vi saw the same awareness in Smith's eyes.

"People get hurt all the time for just being in the way," Smith reminded her. "Maybe right now he's demonizing you to his nephews. Maybe he's saying that you're a rich girl and you've had more than your fair share this whole time. Maybe he's making them swear to do whatever it takes. He doesn't care about you."

Vi nodded and sighed. When they reached the ruins, Vi turned on her torch and stepped into the darkness of the sullen, broken walls.

CHAPTER 16

*a*t first, Vi thought that the ruins were untouched. Then she realized that there were signs, if you knew to look for them. It wasn't so much footprints in the dirt but the utter lack of dirt.

"Why would you sweep?" Vi demanded. "This is so ridiculous."

"They don't want anyone to know that they're puttering around in here." Smith looked around. "They probably are in here as often as they'd like. The old man either didn't know or care."

Vi turned a circle in place. "If you were looking for treasure, where would you look?"

"Here," Rita said sardonically. "Isn't it obvious?"

"Yes," Vi said with a roll of her eyes, "but—"

"But The Goblet of Nemo is ridiculous," Smith said, eyeing the long, broken hallways. "Even I know that and I didn't have your fancy Oxford education."

"Exactly. It sounds like something that dear Edgar would

have scoffed at." Vi turned her torch around the floor and then towards the stone steps that led out.

"Edgar?" Smith demanded, looking beyond Vi to Victor.

Her twin laughed. "If Edgar Rice Burroughs would scoff at The Goblet of Nemo, we should. Vi and I don't adore dear Edgar because he wrote a story of reason. He wrote a story of fluff."

"Brain sweeties," Vi laughed. "That's what Victor and I called them when we were in school. Something to cleanse the palette after a treatise or essays on morality."

"Or, Euclid." Victor shuddered. "The latest Tarzan novel has always been the answer to Euclid."

"Regardless," Smith said, shaking off their joking, "the goblet is ridiculous. It didn't come from these ruins where real people lived, so looking here is also ridiculous. This was a plot, right? A plot of someone who raised that Oscar fellow on nonsense that was so believable to him, so real, he lost his position as a professor."

"Exactly," Vi agreed. "So where would someone hide a supposed treasure whose existence was based off of idiotic stories that they made up on their own? Because whoever didn't tell Oscar it was all a game and let him lose his position and be made a mockery of is a beast."

"Wherever it was hidden, it wasn't here," Smith replied. "The beast knew they'd look here. Anyone looking for treasure that was real would look here. Anyone who was torturing those children would put the treasure somewhere entirely unexpected."

"But somewhere that was obvious," Vi added, leaving the ruins. She wasn't going to waste her time looking for a fantasy that wasn't there. Vi ran up the steps and then stopped suddenly in surprise. "Oh."

"Oh?" Harriet said, her wrinkled hands fisted, her age spots making her seem fragile despite the banked anger in her eyes. "Is that all you have to say?"

Vi's gaze moved to the young man behind Harriet. The old woman and the young man had matching eyes, except that Harriet's were a bit mad. Victor placed his hands on Vi's shoulders, and she knew that he'd try to save her if that young man decided to use the gun in his hand. She'd try to save both of them if she'd thought to have the pistol ready and not tucked into her dress.

"What would you like me to say?" Vi asked. "I assumed you were a kind woman who was willing to help us find the treasure and end all of this."

"That treasure is mine." Harriet glanced towards the younger man and adjusted it to, "Ours."

Vi followed Harriet's gaze, and the young man blushed despite—or maybe because of—the gun he had trained on her.

Vi told him, "You don't want to do this."

"Don't I?" he asked.

"For treasure?" Vi's tone was sufficient to have the young man blushing deeper. "If you hurt us, the constables will be involved, they'll overrun this place, and enough people know about the treasure and your family that they'll find you. Everything will be finished for you then."

"I—"

"John," Harriet snapped. "It's all for you. Oscar and I are old. You deserve better than jumping for every passing partner at your company and scurrying to get them tea and files. Now lift the gun, and we'll lock them in that cellar room and finish our search. We're close. I know it."

Rita stepped out from behind Vi and lifted the elephant

gun to her shoulder. "Shall we have a shootout Old West style? This is the most ridiculous thing I have ever said or done, but if you think I'm going to be locked in a room and left to hope someone will find us, you're wrong."

"You won't shoot us," Harriet told Rita, "you're a sweetheart. You invited a strange woman to live with you. Sweet girls like you probably don't even know how to shoot that gun of yours."

"You invited her to live with you?" Smith asked and Vi glanced at him, noting the knife in his hand. "Why?"

"She's sweet." Rita's tone was defensive and she scowled darkly when Smith snorted.

"I will shoot you where you stand in a half a second to protect my family and friends," Rita told Harriet. "It's not our fault that your grandfather was crazy and played mind games with you the whole of your life. We aren't going to die for that."

"The treasure is real," Harriet told them flatly. "You don't know him. It's real, and it'll change everything for the boys. It'll set their lives aright. I'm going to win against Grandfather. When I see him in the next life, he's going to know I won in the end."

"You know what is the stupidest thing about all of this? We'd have let you look for the treasure if you just asked," Rita told Harriet as she adjusted the gun on her shoulder and clearly moved her finger to the trigger. "Now get off my property and away from my friends."

"Aunt Harriet," the young man said carefully, "we need to go. If constables are pulled in, we're going to have trouble."

"They'll never let us back there, John. If we leave, they'll call the constables and we'll lose everything. We're so close. The treasure is near, I can feel it."

"Is it?" Vi demanded. "How long have you been searching the ruins?"

"My whole life. Of course it's in the ruins. We've dug, we've uncovered the cellars, we've found old out-buildings. Oscar and I know more about this property and what lies here than anyone else ever could. It's just a matter of time."

"And your grandfather was a man of honor?" Vi demanded.

"Are you trying to be funny? Of course he wasn't. He was a first-rate scoundrel, but he always followed the rules of his games. This was his game."

There was something in Harriet's tone that said she had been party to far more games than she had ever wanted even when she'd wanted nothing more than escape.

"Then," Vi told Harriet as though she were dim, "he kept the rules of the game to himself and tricked you into believing false ones."

Harriet stepped back. Her expression had shifted and Vi would guess that Harriet saw the possibility in what Vi had said to her. She'd been tricked and the poor woman recognized it. "Come," she told her nephew. "We must go."

Rita kept the gun on her shoulder as the two left and Victor stepped in front of Vi just in case the duo decided to turn and take a chance in shooting them and continuing their hunt.

"What—" Victor started and then stopped. "I feel bad for her. She thinks you might be right, Vi. If you are, all of those things they discovered about this old place are nothing more than curiosities and a wasted life."

"You probably should feel bad for her," Smith told Victor. "It's what makes you so compelling."

"What?" Victor asked, staring at Smith.

"It's clear that woman's life was dark. You can see it in her. When you aren't treated like you matter, you don't learn that the people around you matter."

"You feel sympathy too, Smith," Rita told him, handing him the elephant gun. "If you didn't, Beatrice wouldn't love you."

"I am not—" Smith started and then groaned. "Why do I put up with you all?"

Victor slapped Smith on the shoulder. "It's all right, old man. You can be the devil among us if you prefer. We'll let Beatrice be the one who knows all your—"

"Please stop," Smith said evenly. He looked in the direction Harriet and her nephew had gone. "That woman has crossed the line to madness. Let's focus on what is important, shall we? Stopping them from murdering us in our sleep because we let down our guard."

Rita sniffed and looked at the ruins behind her. "They saw us come in here."

"Did they?" Victor asked.

"They had their gun at the ready. If they didn't expect us, their weapon would have been hidden."

"How could they know what we're doing?" Victor asked.

"Obviously," Rita snapped, "they're watching us. Do we need to worry about Ham and Jack?"

"No," Victor said immediately. "I hate the idea that they're watching the house." Victor scowled. "My wife is in that house. My daughters. We should call the constables."

"We should," Smith agreed mildly. "But then, of course, we'd be overrun with those looking for this treasure."

"I agree with Smith," Vi said. "We have to find the treasure, discredit its existence, or abandon this place. Otherwise every time Ham and Rita turn around someone will be sneaking in and digging holes or locking them in the house or whatever mad morons do."

Rita glanced towards Vi and then she laughed. "Christmas morning, some idiot in leather pants digging a hole in the orchard, certain he's found the final clue. He's decided the curve on the bottom of the goblet is the tree line or the... the...way the wind flows through the trees."

Vi bit down on her bottom lip, but her own giggles escaped. "So, we don't know this old man. But we do know that he wanted the end of the game to be obvious, right? Or at least we think so."

"He was a sadist," Smith told Vi. "That much is obvious. That woman wouldn't be so mad if he wasn't. That Oscar fellow has to be just as mad."

"Let's telephone the inn," Vi said. "We need Edward Hollands on our side."

"How do we know he isn't working with them? He's Oscar's protégée." Smith didn't sound amused.

"He's not like that," Rita said. "He's an adventure addict. Both of those brothers are. Africa, a rain forest, anywhere that's farther or more dangerous than before."

"Maybe," Violet said, "it is that simple as well. They're not wealthy."

"They aren't. They went with us to Africa because they provided protection and a doctor. We paid the way." Rita shook her head, expression certain. "I know those men. Edward Hollands saved me on that trip. Shelby took care of my friends. They're not bad men. Even in all this, I never suspected they were legitimately involved."

"So, let's pay the way for their trips," Victor said, understanding Vi's thought process immediately. "We could let them go anywhere."

"Why?" Smith shook his head and laughed. "Anywhere, all their trips, just like that?"

"Sure," Victor agreed. "Why wouldn't we?"

"Because, fool," Smith snapped, "they'd help you just for a chance to be there when the treasure is found. They'd do it for a cut of whatever you'd find. They'd do it for a solitary trip. You don't have to go to the far extreme."

"Obviously, fool," Vi told her twin and then laughed when she got a dark look. "You make the call, darling Victor. Apparently, you're the nicest of us."

Vi led the way back towards the house. "Somewhere obvious, Smith. Not the ruins. Not for someone who was taunting them."

"Somewhere nasty," Smith added. "He sold the house and ensured the grandchildren didn't get the goblet. He wanted them to wonder until they died."

Vi paused outside of the house and stared at it. She had to go to the roof to see the line of the river. That was too far. She glanced at Smith. "Where do you think he spent most of his time?"

Smith turned and looked behind him at the ruins and then at Vi. "I think he was right here. Looking out at where they were trying so hard to find the treasure and laughing to himself."

She nodded. "What a sour, awful old man, but I can imagine that so easily."

CHAPTER 17

"I hate that man," Vi told Smith as they walked the line of the house. They examined the view from each window or exit of the house. "Do you think that…"

"Don't think about it," Smith told Vi. "Don't imagine what he might have done. We don't have any idea, and you have quite an imagination. You might streak right past what he did do and ruin your peace with rancid imaginings."

Vi glanced at Smith. Yet again, there was nothing particular in his face that showed him for what he was—good or bad—but he walked at Vi's side, and she was sure that she could trust him.

"It's odd, you know," Vi told him. "When I hired you that first time, when Jack and I needed help and I'd have done anything, anything at all, I never imagined that you'd be one of the few people I trust fully."

"Do you think I deserve that?" Smith asked. His pretty eyes moved relentlessly around the house and Vi had little doubt that he was seeing more than she.

Vi propped herself against the side of the house. She considered a few different options and she told him, "You've been reliable too many times, Smith."

"You do pay me," he told her, as if daring her to deny it.

Vi didn't bother. She took in a deep breath and started away from the house again. She wasn't going to push him. He wasn't her love, but he was her friend, and he deserved better of her. So she started to come up with some common aside that would let them slide back into nonsense when Smith grabbed Vi by the arm, placing a hand over her mouth and backing into the shadows of the house.

Vi froze in Smith's arms, staring up at him and saw his gaze was fixed on the trees on the side of the property.

"Quiet," he hissed and then let go of her mouth. He dropped her arm, and she knew that his knife was in his hand. "Careful."

"Do you have a gun?" Vi breathed. She'd left hers with Victor. Smith shook his head and Vi wondered when they'd become so stupid. She waited only for a moment before she leaned into the shadow of the house and started to sidle sideways. She could hear the sounds of movement in the trees steadily now. Was it possible, she wondered, that it was something easy, like a deer?

The answer was a person stumbling from the trees. Vi gasped, biting off a cry when she saw the person fall to his knees with his hands bound behind his back. It took only a moment to see Jack standing behind the fellow. The look of disgust on Jack's face as he hauled the older man to his feet told Vi that it wasn't the first time Jack had been forced to drag the man back up.

Vi sighed with relief and Smith's smirk chased her from

the shadows to the light. Jack saw the two of them. She grinned at him, and he shook his head.

"Should I be surprised to find you two in the shadows?" he asked as Ham joined them, dragging a younger, bound man with him.

"Bring them," Smith commanded, ignoring the allusion to criminal intent. With Vi it was unlikely but with Smith it was a certainty. "We have questions."

"We're calling the constables," Ham announced. "So get that expectant look off of your face."

"Don't be stupid, Barnes," Smith said to Ham and then his pretty angel eyes flicked to Jack. "You know I'm right."

"You're right?" Vi gasped. "I'm the one who is right. I said from the beginning we needed to find the treasure so we'd stop any further idiots from showing up."

"I'm not going to help you," the old man said, trying and failing to jerk away from Jack. "Why would I help you?"

"I thought you wanted to win against the old man," Smith said. "We assumed you wanted to prove that the theory of The Goblet of Nemo wasn't entirely ridiculous."

"We've been searching for decades," the man told them. "You think we haven't tried whatever it is you think you know?"

"We think," Smith told the man, "that you were searching for the treasure based off of the stories your grandfather told you because he kept the rules of his games. What did he do? Tell you it was real, that he'd seen it, and that it could be yours if you could but find it?"

The stark silence from Oscar and his nephew was enough confirmation.

"Here's the thing, fellows," Smith told them. "You've been

playing the old man's game, and I think we all know that the only winner to that game was him."

"Not if we find it," Oscar said with the desperation of a man who had suspected that he'd been wrong all this time.

"You're a professor," Beatrice said from the side of the house. Her entrance cued everyone else including Victor, who had arrived with the Hollands brothers. They stopped the auto and Edward Hollands saw his old mentor standing in front of the house where the man spent his childhood bound and frustrated.

"Yes," Oscar said.

"Then you must realize that this idea of an ancient treasure is ridiculous."

"But it's not," Edward Hollands cut in. "Oscar—I—I don't know why they've got you bound, but I can guess. Was it you who hit me?"

"You had the goblet." Oscar didn't even sound apologetic. Dr. Hollands examined the ties on Oscar and his nephew's wrists, but the doctor was entirely unbothered.

"What do you mean it's not, Mr. Hollands?" Beatrice asked.

"Oh the goblet is old," Edward told them. "The Nemo name must be a family story, but the goblet itself. It's been around for a long time."

"Jack and I verified that," Ham said.

Vi's head turned among the others and she asked Edward, "Is it likely that there really was a missing fortune?"

Edward nodded immediately. "They were rich. Like you, Mrs. Wakefield. They were remarkably wealthy. Look at this place. What happened to it all?"

"You go back far enough and you'll find people lost fortunes gambling. Or investing in schemes that didn't turn out. They wouldn't have been the first family to lose every-thing. Most have, by now."

"But they didn't," Edward said. "I know you all think I'm an idiot, but I'm not. I heard the stories Oscar told. I followed the money lines, I did the research. They got quite a bit of money in unsavory ways, but they didn't lose it. There wasn't record of an heir who gambled it away. They were the perpetrators of schemes that led to other families' ruins, not theirs."

"Father did pay quite a bit for this house," Rita said. "Where did that money go?"

"He left it to a university," Oscar snapped. "They named a building after him."

"Where did he sit in this house?" Smith suddenly demanded. "Where did he spend his time?"

"Why?" Oscar asked.

Before he could answer they saw Harriet and John step from the trees. Harriet eyed her cousin and then said, "Idiot."

"They hunted us like dogs," Oscar told his cousin. Harri-et's gaze moved over him and then landed on the others.

"It's ours," Harriet told them.

No one agreed, but Beatrice repeated Smith's question.

"Did your grandfather have somewhere he lingered in the house? A favorite room? The library, perhaps?"

"He didn't read," Harriet said. Her eyes were distant, and her memories were clearly haunted. She snapped back to their presence and her lips flattened into a dark scowl. "He tormented us or he drank. Or he did both."

"Where?" Smith demanded with the callousness of a man who had been through his own nightmares.

"The back parlor," Harriet said. "The back parlor where he could see the ruins or us in the garden. Where he could watch us. We weren't allowed in the front of the house. We were to be seen and not heard and if we played at all, we had to play out of sight."

John stepped forward and handed his gun to Violet. "I'm sorry for what we did to you."

Jack watched it all carefully.

Vi looked at the man. "I assume you were doing what you could for them." She gestured at Harriet and Oscar.

It was an exit from the madness he'd been drawn into and John recognized the chance and took it. "Great-grandfather was a monster. Our mother told us stories about him. She refused to let him anywhere near us. Father never once objected to Mother's rules for us."

"She was kinder to you than our parents were to us," Harriet told John. "My brother chose his wife well."

Violet stepped away. She had to. The madness and pain that poured off of Harriet was more than Vi wanted. Instead, she went into the house and moved towards the back parlor and knew that Victor followed. She could almost bet that Jack had shot Victor a look and commanded him to go, but it hadn't been necessary.

"Thank heaven for Aunt Agatha," Victor said and Vi stepped into her brother's arms and shuddered. She didn't have the strength to just dismiss everything as Smith did. After a few stolen moments of comfort, Vi pulled the sketch Kate had made and stepped up to the back parlor. The curving edge of the back patio was there and Vi could easily imagine the malevolent old man watching his grandchildren desperately searching for the treasure.

It wasn't money, Vi thought, that they wanted so badly. Those children had wanted an escape from the man. They'd wanted to win against him, but most of all, they had probably thought, 'With the treasure, I'll finally get away. I'll be able to do what I want to do. I'll be able to—' The particulars didn't matter, Vi thought. In many ways, it had been a mercy to dream and obsess over the supposed fortune. It gave them a hope for the future.

But now? Now Oscar and Harriet were old. They weren't going to have the happily ever after they'd dreamed over. Not after decades of continuing to try to win and failing at each turn.

"You know," Vi said as she stepped into the parlor and examined the room. "It's interesting that it's so verifiable."

"What do you mean?" Victor asked.

"Everyone who has spent any sort of time looking for this fortune is sure it is real."

"Perhaps," Victor suggested, "that's because they want to believe."

Vi took a chair and moved it to the windows. She sat down and then pulled out the map and stared at it. Down and up, back and forth she examined. She sat for well over an hour. Long enough for Jack to check on her. Long enough to hear the sounds of the babies crying. Long enough for Victor to become bored and for Smith to reappear.

Vi watched the others walk about with their own copies of maps. Finally, Vi slowly stood, stretching. "Who gave the goblet its name?"

Smith shook his head in reply. His eyes were fixed on her rather than on the horizon. "What do you know?"

Vi frowned deeply and then crossed to the window and pushed it up, swinging her legs over the edge and then looking back for Smith. "You gave the final necessary clue."

"What clue was that?" Smith demanded.

"I'd never have figured it out without you. The goblet of Nemo. That cranky old man."

"What did you discover? Did you find the line of the map out there?" Smith asked. "I can't see it. I've tried everything I can think of."

"The first problem was ever believing him at all."

CHAPTER 18

*V*iolet summoned everyone to the patio. "I think I might have figured it out."

Harriet scoffed, but given it was only their mercy that had kept them from calling the constables so far, she scoffed quietly. Vi met Jack's gaze and said, "We all agree this whole thing was a game to the old man, right?"

"Right," Jack said, speaking for everyone.

"We've ruled out the ruins simply because they're obvious. Give it enough time and anyone would have found the treasure in the ruins."

"Of course it's in the ruins," Harriet argued. "There's an old map of the great house here. The line of it matched the bottom of the goblet."

Vi shrugged. "But he was a cheater, wasn't he? He didn't play fair."

"You think you know him?" Harriet's voice was a rasp but it wasn't worse than the stark hatred on Oscar's face. "You think you knew what it was like?"

"I think the goblet is a lie."

"A lie?"

"The clue is in the name itself."

"The name is a clue that the treasure belongs to nobody," Oscar said, sounding exhausted. "You aren't the only one who can figure out the Latin meaning of a word and realize that Grandfather called the goblet that for a reason. It was the promise of his blasted treasure hunt."

"It's named so for two reasons," Vi told Oscar. "The one you ferreted out and one other."

"What is the other?" Harriet asked. Her gaze almost roiled. If Harriet had been a weather pattern, lightning would be streaking across the sky.

Vi looked down at the patio where she stood, her gaze focused on the curve of the patio. "This was added later."

Both Oscar and Harriet froze.

Vi walked along the line of the patio. It was just brick. Someone had done a good job with it. It had been expensive, Vi thought. It had been expensive and right there in front of them all the whole time. The old man was a sadistic creep. He was the type of man to sell his house and leave his fortune to a school, so he could have a building named after him. He was the kind of man whose daughter-in-law protected her children from him, regardless of the money.

He was the kind of man who added a patio, hid his money, and then started a treasure hunt after. What children wouldn't look in the ruins for buried treasure?

But the addition right there in front of them? How could they begin to suspect?

Vi walked the patio, staring down and when she found it she wasn't even surprised.

A carved X on a pillar at the edge of the patio near the

steps. X for nobody. X for treasure. And right there in front of their eyes every time they walked out of the house and towards the ruins.

On either side of the steps down to the garden there was a stone lion on a pedestal. Vi's fingers moved easily over the statue with the X and she found the switch just by the lion's great paw, looking like a missed cut in the stone.

A moment after she pushed it, there was the sound of stone moving against stone and a small entrance on the house opened up. Just beneath the back parlor, right in the side of the old house, a hidden entrance led down to the cellars.

At first, no one moved. Then gasps of shock and confusion. Oscar demanded to see the button. Harriet made for the discovered door, but Ham caught her.

Smith and Jack went first with the torch, but Vi didn't. She stayed outside as everyone, including the surviving members of the old man's family, went to find the treasure.

Rita hesitated at the entrance. "Don't you want to know what is in there?"

Vi shook her head and took a seat on a nearby bench. After a glance at the gaping doorway, Rita crossed to sit next to her friend. Vi laid her head on Rita's shoulder.

"What if it's pirate gold?" Rita's voice was filled with humor, but neither of them were actually amused.

"I'll know how to describe it for my book." Vi squeezed Rita's hand.

"Should I hate this place now?" Rita asked without any attempt at humor. "We've learned too much about its past."

"No," Vi said. "This isn't the hot bed of our nightmares. It's theirs."

Rita sighed. "I suppose you're right. I could say that bad things happened here. Only that's true of any old house."

Their friends started filing out of the room and Vi and Rita looked their question.

"Quite a nasty letter," Beatrice told them.

"And a key," Smith added. "It goes to a bank box in London. They can gather whatever was left there."

"Shall we call the constables now?" Rita asked Ham.

"They're leaving," he told her. "They've sworn never to return. We won't be so kind next time."

"I can't believe we found it," Edward cheered. He raised his hands overhead and then slapped his brother on the back. "Now I can stop wondering."

"But you aren't going to get any of the treasure," Vi told him.

"Oh, I would have taken some if I could have." Edward grinned wickedly with a look for his brother. "We'd have just sold it and gone to the Amazon. Now, however, your brother is financing our trip to the Amazon, so we got what we wanted after all."

"They have quite large snakes there," Rita told them. "As I recall, you're a baby about snakes, Hollands."

Neither brother replied. Instead, they rounded the side of the house and watched as Ham got rid of the intruders and turned back to everyone else.

"I suppose I have to feed you," Ham said.

Vi rolled her eyes and rose, crossing to Jack and snuggling into his side. "I'd rather go home."

That was all he needed to take her by the hand and lead her to the automobile. On the way back to their house, she asked, "What do you think they'll find?"

Jack shook his head and then admitted, "Whatever it is,

it's not payment enough for the life they led or the time they lost."

Vi tangled her fingers with Jack's and laid her head on his shoulder.

"You know what the treasure is for us?"

He waited for her answer, but she knew that he did know. The treasure was the realization of how lucky they were. They had parents who loved them. They had what they needed. They had happy childhoods and they had eventually found each other. It was so easy to joke they were cursed, but how could anyone be cursed who was so loved?

"What would your pirate werewolf say to his princess about the treasure?" Jack asked.

"He'd lift his love in his arms," Vi told Jack, "and carry her to their bed and whisper into her ear, 'You're my treasure.'"

Jack laughed. But when they returned home, he did just that.

The END

HULLO FRIENDS! I am so grateful you dove in and read the latest Vi and friends mystery. If you wouldn't mind, I would be so grateful for a review.

THE SEQUEL to this book is available is now available.

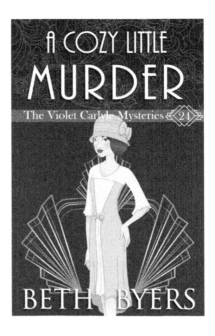

September 1926.

Vi and Jack have settled into London for the fall, and they want nothing more than an excess of cocoa, coffee, good books, and time with friends.

They should, however, know better. Jack is brought into consult on a case in coziest of houses. Only all is not what it seems and no one is surprised when they find yet another body.

Order your copy here.

MYSTERY at the Edge of Madness is the first in a new series.

October 1925

Severine DuNoir was twelve when she discovered the bodies of her parents, and the day after the funeral, she was sent to a convent in another country. By the time she resolves to go home, her sole focus is to reveal what happened to her parents.

Coming home, however, unveils a far more sinister plot than she could have expected. It's clear from her first night that something is afoot. The motives are many and the target is clear: Severine herself.

Order your copy here or keep on scrolling to read the first chapter.

PREVIEW OF THE MYSTERY AT THE EDGE OF MADNESS

CHAPTER ONE

"I don't understand," Severine said, feeling particularly dim.

The gentleman smiled kindly. "I'm your guardian." He had said it more than once, and his tone and delivery had turned slow to the point of speaking to someone who wasn't quite capable of understanding.

It wasn't that she didn't know he was her guardian. Of course, she did. Regardless of her confusion, she was not an idiot. She'd heard of the mysterious Mr. Brand who watched over her inheritance in trust, but she hadn't expected *this* fellow. He was not that much older than she. She'd expected a life-long school chum of her father or perhaps one of his mentors. A much older man filled with wisdom and a shared *history* with her father.

That was the key factor. Severine would turn eighteen in two days. This fellow had to be in his late twenties. Which meant, given her parents had died almost exactly six years ago, that he had control of the DuNoir estate when he was barely old enough to have his legal majority. He looked as if he were a mere year or two older than herself, so how had he looked six years before? The fellow had pale, nearly white, blonde hair, the sort of pale skin that showed every passing emotion with the shade of red he turned, and the blue eyes that revealed his thoughts. He was tallish, broad-ish, thin-nish, and handsome-ish. He was very medium, Severine thought. Unremarkable really, except for that pale, pale skin, which wasn't very remarkable to her considering her own pale, pale skin.

"Your father came to me just before he died, and he asked me to look after you. We had quite a long conversation, really."

Her father, who had two brothers, business partners, a best friend, and a slew of friends, had discussed her with him when this man was barely a legal adult himself..

Severine took a deep breath. "It's not that I don't under-stand your words," Severine repeated. "It's that I have a half-brother who could have served if Father was going to choose someone so young."

"Your father didn't want your brother to look after you. He wanted you to have your freedom. Your half-brother is of quite a different cloth than I am."

"But Father didn't love me. Mother either." Her gaze moved to the convent where she'd lived since her parents' death. Being raised in a convent didn't inspire one to imagine a future of early freedom, let alone control of her inheritance and the two houses.

He coughed and avoided her gaze as he cleared his throat and blushed enough for her to be sure that Mr. Brand had suspected the same thing she'd known since before she could read.

"Perhaps rather than trying to understand your father's reasoning," Mr. Brand suggested softly, "we can accept him at his word. He wanted you to be safe as you grew up and be free of the meddling of his friends and relatives."

"Father was murdered," Severine told him precisely.

"He was," the man said, looking sympathetic but without answering.

Why! Severine wanted to shout, but she guessed this man was being purposefully vague. He wasn't looking at her at the moment. He was staring at the statue of Mary and baby Jesus in the garden and taking in the magnificent stained-glass windows. He was avoiding her gaze and side-stepping her questions and offering her the money that belonged to her, without explaining why her father had come up with such an irregular future for her—all just before he had been murdered.

She knew the answer of course: because he had known he was going to die. Or suspected it enough to put plans into place. Plans that meant her father hadn't been sure of any of the regular choices for guardian. Which suggested, Severine thought with a sudden chill, that she could trust no one.

She listened without commenting as her guardian explained that she would have control of her money, of the houses, of all of it, the moment she returned to the United States. He finished with, "Your father said he trusted you to look after yourself, the fortune he was leaving you, and the accoutrements of being a DuNoir."

She didn't repeat that she'd been a disappointment to her parents. Even her name, which they tried to make a joke of later, had been a glaring symbol of that disappointment. Father had told her the story once.

"*Sevie*," he had said, using the nickname she'd despised

even at ten years old. *"We expected you to enter the world screaming. I was prepared to laugh indulgently, press a kiss on your sweet forehead, and tell your mama what a good job she'd done, but you were the most serious little thing I had ever seen— looking as though you were possessed by Lady Justice."*

That had been when he'd laughed nervously. *"It's why we named you Severine, of course. So serious from the moment you entered the world."*

Severine snapped back to the present, completely having missed whatever nonsense the man had been telling her.

When she focused back to him, he blushed again lightly. He cleared his throat a few more times and said, "So, you'll need me to sign off on things until you're twenty-one, but for all intents and purposes, you'll be making the choices. I promised your father that you could make your own way— regardless of my opinion on the matter. That's a promise I intend to keep."

Severine hesitated and then demanded, "Why?"

"Your father saved my life during the war." For once Mr. Brand didn't avoid her gaze. "I'd have seen him live a long and full life if I had my wish. I didn't, but I'll be"—those blue eyes settled on the statue of Mary and he censored himself— "darned if I don't keep my promise to him."

Well, Severine thought, that made sense at least. A man who seemed to be one of honor. One who wasn't connected with Father's business practices. Who was old enough to stand for her father and beholden enough to him to just do as he wanted. Was this the *only* man her father had trusted Severine with?

Severine rocked back on her heels. "So if I wanted to go home—"

~

SEVERINE EUPHRASIA DUNOIR stared at herself in the mirror and saw a stranger. Her face was all sharp angles and high cheekbones. It was what it was, she thought, having vanity thoroughly scoured from her in her youth and then completely buried with living in a convent for six years. She would never be lovely like her mother, and that had been the only useless wish of Severine's heart when she'd bothered to make wishes. She had once wanted to be pretty and frivolous and as loved as her mother, and she had accepted it would never happen.

The days of useless fairy wishes were long past for Severine and she was stolidly something else. She met the gaze of the shop girl and asked, "Is this a normal dress?"

The dress reached mere inches below her knees, and Severine's dark brown eyes were fixed on her naked legs. Her legs weren't actually naked given the stockings, but she certainly felt as scandalous as Godiva on her nude horseback ride after all. The dress was a soft pink that made her want to vomit as she took in her white skin against the color. She looked like a blushing ghost.

She felt naked and ridiculous. Women wore such things here? Clearly, however, they did. The shop girl looked lovely and vivacious. Her pretty dark-brown locks were cut quite close to her head and smoothed into curls that clung to her forehead and cheek. While Severine thought it was quite flattering on the girl, she was sure it would never do for herself, even if one didn't take into account the difference in their hair texture. The shop girl seemed to be of mulatto descent and had the Creole accent of so many in New Orleans. Severine's mouth twisted. She had a goal, and that goal required she look the part of one of these bright young things. She had accepted she'd never be frivolous like her mother, so how was she to accomplish her goal?

"This is a normal dress," the shop girl said gently. "Where you been, cher? The moon?"

Severine paused and admitted, "Almost." She tried for cheery but failed.

"And people don't bob their hair where you were? Or—" The girl gestured to the dress rather than explaining. Her horrified gaze was enough for Severine to laugh, but she was positive her humor didn't really appear on her face.

"Oh." Severine hesitated, her mouth twisting. "No. Not really."

"Well, hello, darlin'," the girl said cheerily, drawing out the hello. "Welcome to the new world."

Severine tried and failed for another smile, but it seemed the attempt was sufficient. Or perhaps the warmth that appeared in the girl's eyes was from what Severine said next.

"I need to change my look. You seem…" Severine struggled for the words and then hoped that ready money would make up for inarticulate words. "Quite modern and…" Another awkward pause until Severine added, "Quite fashionable. Lovely. So many of the others I've been watching look as though they're parroting the fashion, while you look as though you're setting it."

It was the right thing to say. The girl held out her hand and said, "Meline Boucher. Fashion *is* my passion. I hope to have my own shop with my own line someday."

They considered dress after dress and then Meline's head tilted as she said, "I think we need to embrace you as you are, cher. Putting you in a rose dress and bobbing your hair will make you look like a penguin wearing peacock feathers."

Severine waited for Meline to explain, but instead the woman disappeared into the back. She returned with sketch papers and a pencil box. In moments, Meline was sketching in black pencil and Severine was watching with interest as her face and her form appeared on the paper.

Dress after dress filled the pages that followed. Some of the dresses were black on black. Some were dark gray with black embroidery. One was a black and red wine that reached from chest to the floor and even had something of a train. Severine, for the first time in her life, desperately wanted the dresses on those pages.

When Meline paused drawing, Severine asked, "How long?"

Meline paused and then offered a date that was too far away.

"Is it possible to have them in two weeks? Perhaps if you hire help?"

Meline paused and then nodded, a slow, excited grin crossing her face. "I'll get fired for certain if Madam," she said it like an insult, "realizes that I've taken on a job like this."

"Then, let's not tell her. Let's find something that will do for now, and we'll meet at my house for the rest. I'll need sensible day dresses and skirts with pockets along with this look. Can you make that happen as well?"

Meline nodded quickly.

Severine wrote her address on a page with her name and left the shop. When she stepped back onto the bustling streets of New Orleans, she winced. There were people *everywhere.* Handsome, fashionable, hard-working. There was a scent in the air, and Severine flashed back to a random afternoon in her childhood when her father had brought her to a ramshackle place that served beignets and chicory coffee. He'd let her have both, though she'd been too young for coffee, and she'd dared to dunk her beignet in the coffee just as her father did.

He'd grinned wide and she'd seen a little of herself in his face. His sharp jawline perhaps, or those dark eyes that were almost black.

Maybe he hadn't disliked her, but she'd never know. Her eyes burned with something that was more complicated than grief. Her parents had been murdered before she could know them, and it had changed her forever.

IF YOU ENJOYED THIS, click here for more.

ALSO BY BETH BYERS

THE VIOLET CARLYLE COZY HISTORICAL
MYSTERIES

(This series is ongoing.)

Murder & the Heir

Murder at Kennington House

Murder at the Folly

A Merry Little Murder

Murder Among the Roses

Murder in the Shallows

Gin & Murder

Obsidian Murder

Murder at the Ladies Club

Weddings Vows & Murder

A Jazzy Little Murder

Murder by Chocolate

A Friendly Little Murder

Murder by the Sea

Murder On All Hallows

Murder in the Shadows

A Jolly Little Murder

Hijinks & Murder

Love & Murder

A Zestful Little Murder

A Murder Most Odd

Nearly A Murder

A Treasured Little Murder

A Cozy Little Murder

Masked Murderer

Meddlesome Madness: A short story collection

Silver Bells & Murder

Murder at Midnight

A Fabulous Little Murder

Murder on the Boardwalk

THE MYSTERIES OF SEVERINE DUNOIR

The Mystery at the Edge of Madness

The Mysterious Point of Deceit

Mystery in the Darkest Shadow

The Wicked Fringe of Mystery

The Lurid Possibility of Murder

The Uncountable Price of Mystery

The Inexorable Tide of Mystery

THE POISON INK MYSTERIES

(This series is complete.)

Death By the Book

Death Witnessed

Death by Blackmail

Death Misconstrued

Deathly Ever After

Death in the Mirror

A Merry Little Death

Death Between the Pages

Death in the Beginning

A Lonely Little Death

THE 2ND CHANCE DINER MYSTERIES

(This series is complete.)

Spaghetti, Meatballs, & Murder

Cookies & Catastrophe

Poison & Pie

Double Mocha Murder

Cinnamon Rolls & Cyanide

Tea & Temptation

Donuts & Danger

Scones & Scandal

Lemonade & Loathing

Wedding Cake & Woe

Honeymoons & Honeydew

The Pumpkin Problem

THE HETTIE & RO ADVENTURES

cowritten with Bettie Jane
(This series is complete.)

Printed in Great Britain
by Amazon